THE 20TH CENTURY SURVIVORS' CLUB

WBR JEREMY

THE DIAMOND CAT PRESS

CONTENTS

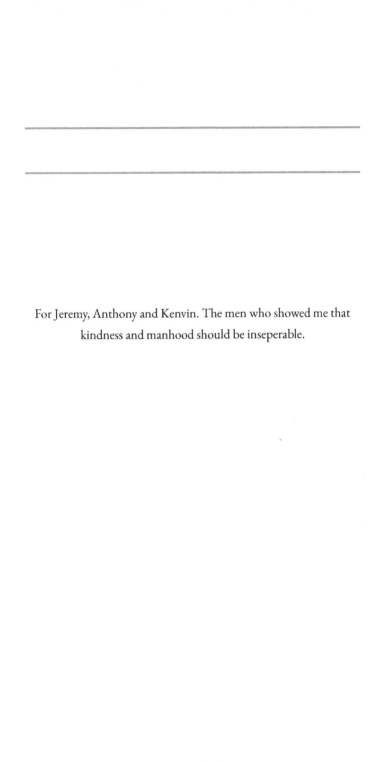

For Jeremy, Anthony and Kenvin. The men who showed me that
kindness and manhood should be inseperable.

INTRODUCTION

" There are fortunate men to whom life is a continuous developing pattern, whose education leads them on to a career......

" No such life has been mine. For to me and thousands like me, that easy developing pattern was completely thrown out of symmetry by the First World War. But we were very young, had no place actual or prospective, in a peaceful world. We walked off the playing-fields into the lines. We lived supremely in the moment. We were trained with one object – to kill. We had one hope – to live.

" When it was over we had to start again... in moments

of depression, when I wish for a longer sweep to carry me safely into the sober years and that, strangely, it eludes me, I console myself with the futile reflection: 'it's the War my boy, it's the War'. "

Cecil Lewis, *Sagittarius Rising* (1937)

CHAPTER ONE

They came from across the country and from across the world; old and young, rich and poor, figures from the past and the all-too intrusive present. Very old men supported by walking sticks and held up by women of indeterminate age ranging from long-suffering wife to sprightly granddaughter via the odd companion who once would have been called a mistress, but in these days of language moderation that term no longer could be used. They came by car in such numbers, that the warden of the church in Cholet St Lawrence lost his usual savoir faire and calm until one of the more organised of the village ladies suggested they open the village hall carpark and tempted the more boisterous of the youth by the promise of high-vis jackets and some cash in hand to organize the parking. Just before 11 o'clock, a phalanx of cars arrived and assorted figures climbed out. They looked to village eyes, familiar yet from both yesterday and the day before, as Mrs. Percombe who knew about the way the world turned, or so she said with force and regularity, pointed out afterwards. Men, in the main, whom the papers used to call captains of industry. Retired military personnel, civil servants, journalists and the odd bestselling author of popular history. A television interviewer from the glorious early days of the medium. Some equally nostalgic media executives exchanging hail-fellow well meant to pensioned-off counterparts in aviation. A clutch, or perhaps, a conspiracy of former leading politicians who huddled in a gossip-starved group, back-slapping and anecdote-swapping.

They came, watched by a young man in best blazer, cords and roll-neck black sweater doing his best to hold back the tears with a voice in his head redolent of adventure and an old-world gravelly charm admonishing him. "People die Hamish, and you'll just have to get used to it." He couldn't get used to it and who *were* all these people? JAK was his, Hamish's, friend, his companion next door for storytelling and afternoon coffee at weekends or quick visits after school before being dragged away by insistent grown-ups saying that, "You must not bother the man next door or you'll tire him out – he's old and ill and doesn't want you hanging around."

Hamish said in reply that JAK didn't mind, they were friends. The grown-ups looked at each other and changed the subject. For they were indeed friends, the old man and the young, and theirs was a friendship across time and space – a lot of time and a good deal of space indeed, bridged by a love of storytelling and the acceptance and understanding that only the very old and the young can have.

Hamish would at times, enthused by his love of history, suggest that JAK should write some of these tales down, especially his life story. "O no, dear boy, no-one would be in the remotest bit interested in my story. Too much water under the bridge, too many other things to do and think about without conjuring up the dead, you know!" Hamish tried to imagine what "other things to do" JAK had in mind, confined as he was to a wheelchair, mobile only with the aid of a walker with a carer into his small cottage twice a day. Then one day excited with an idea that JAK was bound to leap at, Hamish arrived for late afternoon tea with a small device in his hand. "I've been thinking, JAK. You don't need to write anything down, what with your hands and everything being tricky. You can talk into this phone recorder and I can do the writing for you!" For a moment the light of connection and recognition for a wonderful plan leapt into JAK's piercing blue eyes, not yet clouded by rheum or cataract. "Of course, what a wonderful idea, dear boy, shall do...show me how it works...reminds me of the first of the fangled devices back in the day...." Then JAK's flow of bonhomie stopped. He looked at the clock, declared that it was past supper time and bed, and in his customary way would smile at Hamish, sending him home with a, "Tomorrow is a new adventure, we start afresh..." No more was said of the phone-recorder – Hamish, disappointed but reconciled to JAK's resistance left the device with him and said no more about it. The stories would flow when JAK felt well and in Hamish, he had a ready, willing, and beguiled listener. The very old man telling his tale and the young man entranced. And so, the seasons rolled by and this late life relationship blossomed.

One day, as it must, it all came to an end. As Shakespeare once said, "our little lives are rounded in a sleep."

On a dull Wednesday afternoon, Hamish came back from school bursting with something he had been told by Mr. Frobisher the history teacher about the First World War which he wanted to share with JAK. He arrived in time to see an ambulance driving away from JAK's cottage. Hamish ran up the path, to find the carer who had got quite fond of the old man, tidying up in the small, cramped kitchen. "O young Hamish, bad news I'm afraid. Shortly after lunch, Mr. JAK sat in his chair, turned on the radio, leaned back, settling in for the afternoon. Looking forward to seeing you, he was. I went to boil the kettle for coffee, the next minute he was gone. Had to call an ambulance. A heart attack they said I am so sorry..." Hamish stood there, numb, delayed reaction preventing an immediate response.

Since then, the days took on an automated rhythm. Arrangements were made, people bustled about, strangers took over proceedings and Hamish did not know how to respond. A man of about 60 arrived two days after JAK 'passed.' "I hate euphemisms for death, Hamish, dear fellow. People die, they are not 'lost' or 'pass on.' The good Lord does not mop their brow. He seizes them." Hamish, however, did feel lost. The man claimed to be related to JAK, indeed said he was his nephew, who lived two hours drive away and could not get down 'as easily as I might.' JAK had never talked of any family. He would say when Hamish asked, "Ah, that is quite another saga and not one for this afternoon, perhaps another time, dear boy..." Hamish felt this person had no right to state he was any relation to JAK. He, Hamish, would have been told, would know. After all, he and JAK were the best of friends. JAK had told him so. And why was there a For Sale sign outside JAK's house?

Yanked back to the present, a grieving Hamish stood sentinel at the back of the church as all these people. Who were they, filling into the Norman village church? JAK had not been a regular attender, so the vicar chose his own favourite hymns that he thought might be suitable at the funeral of a very old man, precise age unknown: *Love Divine all Loves Excelling*; *Jerusalem the Golden* and *Glorious Things of Thee Are Spoken*. At the moment when the vicar had planned to give an address complete with plea for donations to the spire restoration fund, there came a voice from deep in the middle pews. "Excuse me

Vicar, but we cannot let this occasion pass without some words being said." The voice was what middle 20th Century novelists of the class system in England would describe as 'cut-glass' and belonged to the tall, imposing, elegant figure of a woman used to the company of men and able to hold her own. Some present in the assembled company were convinced it was Dame Clarissa Joan of Television fame. This figure rose from her place, sidled to the edge of the pew and made her way to the lectern.

Hamish stood astonished. The lady addressed the assembled company as if it were the most natural thing in the world to be speaking in front of those who regard themselves as representatives of the great and the good.

"Look, I know this seems quite irregular and no doubt it is. We cannot let this event go past without words. The good Lord, and all of us, knows how fond of words he was. If there is one thing I know about JAK, it is that. After all, as some here may be aware, I was once, madly, joyfully, impossibly, married to him. You will all have memories of him, worked with him, adventured with him, loved him, envied him, been frustrated and admiring of him all at once. A century is a long time, almost perhaps, beyond time for a human being. Where would anecdotes get us? Where would stories of who said what, when and how? After so long, does it matter where the secrets are hidden? Who is to say what a good life well lived consists of? All we know for sure is that we do not know anything for sure. Perhaps the poet John Donne had it right when pointing out that we are not islands. As Donne says, "For I am in the business of mankind" and so *in excelsis* was JAK. Another poet Karl Luedtke puts into words the sentiment that JAK would perhaps approve of before saying, 'Of course, you do know that it is all stuff and nonsense and we are all atoms and dust, atoms and dust.' I might add, he said that on our wedding night and when we parted. So, now take back the soul of Jeremy Anthony Kenvin Tilyard. He gave us joy. We loved him well. He was not ours, or yours or mine forever. We will miss him. He is too precious to do without. But we must try. For in due time, we'll have to learn to do so. And not cry."

From his vantage point at the back of the church, Hamish finally let go. He allowed the tears that he had been keeping at bay to flow, down both cheeks and into his roll-neck collar. He didn't mind. He resisted the urge to run down the length of the church and embrace this rather forbidding lady, shouting "Yes! Another friend of JAK – you get it!" But he did not. Then unexpectedly, instead of going back to her place in the pews the Dame of Television walked purposefully down the aisle towards Hamish, took his hand in hers and stood there whilst the vicar announced the closing hymn. They stood together, in silent acknowledgment and mutual understanding. No words were needed. Hamish knew that this woman knew – she just *knew*. It was enough. Their moment together counted and chronological time would last for as long as the hymn took to sing, and in Hamish's heart for the rest of his life. "Savior if of Zion's City, I through grace a member am...".

The temporary congregation did not stay for the burial. It was as if all that had to be done had been done. All the representatives of the great and the good filed out of the church into the winter sun in groups as they had come in, now released to include laughter with their glances amidst the hubbub of conversation. In silent complicity and empathy, not exchanging a word but the certain knowledge of two souls who had loved JAK, Hamish in the manner of a gentleman knight of old, walked Dame Television to her car, ignoring the throng waiting to have chats with his charge and brushing off the looks of once–important men who in their turn asked, albeit silently on their tongues but loudly in their minds. "Who is that young chap?" Before she took her seat in the back of the car, she squeezed his hand, gave him an unexpected kiss, and uttered some last words which would sustain Hamish in the time to come. "We did him proud, you and me. Go well and thank you". And then she was gone.

The door closed; the car accelerated away. It was done. Or so he thought.

CHAPTER TWO

The magic began after that in an unexpected way. On returning home, not having the heart to go back to the graveside or the appetite for funeral finger food, Hamish found a package marked with his name on it sitting on the kitchen table. A note from the kind carer – a condolence card inscribed: "found in Mr. JAK's effects, thought you should have it, hope it is in order." His heart raced; his nerves tingled. Why? "People die, Hamish." He heard in his ear, clear as a bell, "but life is for the living...." Hamish opened the package. In it was the phone recorder he had given JAK in youthful hope, those few years ago. With it were tapes, marked in a shaky, arthritic hand: "JAK Tilyard – my story: for Hamish, the boy who cared to ask."

Hamish sat there quivering with a mixture of apprehension, astonishment and excitement to leaven his grief and bewilderment that his friend JAK was no longer with him but there, folded into the piece of technology he held in his hands. Dare he start? A familiar voice in his ear. "Fresh adventures, my boy, fresh adventures." He loaded the first tape and pressed play. It was as if JAK sat in his chair again, blue eyes sparkling, neckerchief at his throat tied in a carefree manner, thinning dark hair swept back from his forehead, large expressive hands punctuating the air to reinforce the point, the crested gold signet ring on the last finger of his left hand ('only place a gentleman should wear jewellery, dear chap') glinting in the dying light of the day. The voice – that voice which had bewitched him for so long filling the room with its promise of adventure and lost worlds, once again belonged to Hamish and Hamish alone.

"Dear boy, first of all an apology. Your idea for a chronicle was first class but you see I got cold feet, rather worried about bringing people long dead to life and not knowing the effect. Actually, it was Gladys, my name for the daily, who sparked me again, if truth – and we are at last in the truth business – were told. In her typical off-hand manner, which can at times be irritating as I am sure you know, she said words akin to 'gosh Mr. JAK, I sometimes can't help over-hearing what you are telling that boy next door, filling his head with all those tales. Can they be true or are you just being kind to a lonely youngster?' Being kind! Not true, tale telling! Impertinence, thy name is woman, I thought. And then I remembered the recorder. Perhaps it was time to set the record straight. One thing I have got, as is my burden to be reminded every day, is *time*. I don't mind admitting that it does hang heavy between your visits, old fruit. I suppose it is something of a saga. That Welsh poet chappie, Dylan Thomas, put it rather well when he said, what was it, "to begin at the beginning…""

"I was born on the first day of January 1900. The dawn of a new century. A Victorian by a matter of months. Conceived by chance, to astonished and aging parents in the 19th Century and born in some difficulty with the aid of a passing obstetrician in the 20th. My put-upon mother, God rest her soul, carried me through the long winter of the last year of the 19th Century, a burden which should never have been placed on a woman then, as the Americans say, crowning 40. Well, despite the potential for Victorian melodramas, I survived and so did she, her only and much adored yet held at arms-length, which was the custom of the time. There were no siblings to grow up alongside, play roughhouse and knock-about with, no older brother to idealise, no sisters to adore. It was me, my outgoing and rather progressive suffragette mother, wedded to causes and parties and my cold, observant-eyed but warm-hearted writer father, sometime lawyer and poor businessman with a hospitable disposition and the wish for money upon which to express that bonhomie part of his nature. We had money from time to time, depending on the client at the door and the publication in hand. A house in Berkshire bought from the proceeds of an old aunt's will on my mother's side, with the accompanying delights of a garden but no extensive resource to entertain on the scale they would have wished. They managed to fill my childhood home with people, laughter, music, conversation. They built castles in the air, those two love birds, who found themselves unexpectedly with a son and a dwelling in the country. My name caused a minor sensation amongst the burghers of the county that gloried in its name Royal Berkshire. The murmurs of the cognoscenti when news spread that a boy had been christened with Jeremy as his given name at the font before the full gaze of the parish – large ladies in larger hats tutting with disapproval. Who are these people? The social calm was hardly restored when my two supporting names were announced: Anthony and Kenvyn – a much adored Welsh great-uncle on my father's side. The word to describe it, so I am led to believe as the assembled congregation trotted out into the brisk Berkshire village air shaking heads and bustling was 'louche'. The new arrivals in Halls Lane were immediately badged as, 'unconventional, bohemian, slightly odd'."

If boyhood was idyllic, schooling was less so, but not oppressive. I grew tall, was deemed clever, diffident yet called 'gifted' in racquet sports, on the river or in the classroom. We had little of what men with moustaches and worried frowns called 'capital' but more of what they rather disapprovingly referred to as 'cash-flow,' when business affairs fared fine. I later learned that this was a feature of what the social observers called 'genteel poverty'. I knew it as life – I never wanted and went without but was aware of a hierarchic system which always left me baffled and not a little bewildered. This was counter-balanced by the seemingly ceaseless flow of people in and out of the house throughout my childhood and youth: artists, writers, actors, adventurers, politicians, journalists – assorted 'clients' of one kind or another. I was never excluded from their company and from a young age would sit listening, clad in pyjamas and dressing gown at first then in the universal schoolboy attire of shorts, cap and blazer, to the conversation of deep-throated men talking often with heavy crystal glass in one hand and a cigar in the other, and women with delightful smiles and delighted laughter. The life-long appreciation of the magic of conversation and the thrill of the human voice telling a story, in song or talk was born of these encounters.

Our family lack of 'capital means' was to prove, eventually, a gift and not a burden in one particular, and very personal way. It was obvious from the start that I could not benefit from a conventional boys schooling at a boarding establishment, which would have been the natural destination, due to lack of funds. It would be scholarships all the way and making the best of what would be at that time universally acknowledged as a 'second division' school. There was no lack of friends, advisors, business associates offering to pay the fees for one of the 'classic' public schools. My parents were adamant that, generous as these offers were and kindly meant, they could not contemplate being what they regarded as 'beholden' to anyone else for my education. So, it was not Eton, Harrow, Winchester, Charterhouse or even Cheltenham College I was sent, courtesy of a moustachioed benefactor. It was Hopkins School, near Reading, on a racquets-academic scholarship. Not only a Quaker establishment but no cadet force, a considerable irony considering what was to come. And a day boy to boot, as the fees would be even further reduced.

As it turned out, these were happy, perhaps even blissful days. The unusual approach taken by the school meant the culture of a minor public school mixed with the devotion to learning and matters of the mind of an enlightened grammar school. Sports were to the fore, as if to make up for the lack of martial cadets, but I was permitted to grace the tennis, squash, and racquets court and occasionally the rowing eight would draft my services. I was neither rugger bugger nor flannelled fool. I accomplished everything early, as befitted my height and what an over-lyrical history master christened my 'old-world head in the clouds.' Destined it seemed for a life in the library and study, of writing and contemplation with bursts of action on court or river, I discovered aviation aged 16, and fell in love. A client of my fathers with a pre-war plane provided the scene of my attachment and machines, later to be described as constructed of 'plywood and chewing gum.'

The conflict in Europe which was sparked by an assassination in Sarajevo and descended into the stalemated trench-ridden calamity on what became known as the Western Front, had been ongoing since 1914. My grades were top, my school record perfect, my manner respectful yet bouncy and out-going – a certain boyish charm was the phrase an encouraging head wrote in a birthday card on the occasion of my 17th birthday – adding the rider, "we shall have to be careful or lose him to the air." I begged, borrowed, and stole time to escape the obligations that took a successful schoolboy's time in those far-off days, for I was too young for high school office and too advanced for school certificate which I had passed through with what masters at the time insisted on calling 'flying colours' even when at the most non-military of establishments. The deal was that I could take leave of class-room absence during the day to pursue 'outside interests' as long as I honoured sporting, chapel, social, house play and other school-based commitments when teaching was done. A certain number of hours were laid aside for me to attend the sixth form scholarship class – they had high hopes for me at a place amongst those 'dreaming spires' of Oxford or Cambridge Universities. What a later-century writer would call the "glittering prizes" were deemed to be within my reach. It was not to be, but not for want of spirit on my part or encouragement on the part of masters and parents.

So, the pull of adventure was irresistible. My fate, as with so much of that which governs the unintended, was determined by the fact that I seemed to be a 'natural' Those with wiser heads and sadder hearts had a feeling for the inevitable. The roster of those personages included my parents, my history master and encourager-in-chief and the headmaster who had such high hopes of an Oxbridgian scholar.

The turn of the year 1918 brought with it an 18[h] birthday and the closer awareness of the sound of the heavy guns on the Western Front that when the wind blew in a certain direction could be clearly heard from many points across Southern England. All I knew was that I wanted to fly, and I wanted to serve, to do 'my bit'. I also knew that I would have to persuade a reluctant head and then my parents to approve my decision to leave school early. I felt a man but, in most things, I was still a boy and even in company as enlightened for the age as my parents and my schoolmasters, I was a still a youth under authority of elders.

I broke my headmaster's heart with my trademark boyish smile and exuberant manner. The place was his study, and the time was that called by Anglican clergyman, Evensong. It was early in the summer term. Mr. Robertson-Rhodes had asked me to pop in to see him 'when my timetable both curricular and extra permitted.' I did not climb the stairs to his lofty eyrie high above the school yard with trepidation or anxiety. He was no tyrant. Yet his autocracy – for all heads of school were in those days' absolute rulers of their kingdoms – was based on force of personality, the Matthew Arnold philosophy of 'sweetness and light' and the rare but ferocious use of temper only when no other course was available. The breaking of my unintended and unknowing vow went thus:

"Ah, Tilyard, come in. How goes it? I trust I am not keeping you from air, book, river or court! Activities both curricular or otherwise? The books may have to be attended to a little more frequently if University entrance is to be achieved, what say you?

"But Sir, the War...."

"What of the War? We know the how's and whys and wherefores, the stupidities, the vainglories, the waste! You have had the most international of educations here, young man. You know more than most that this carnage will end badly and reflect on all the participants in it and to it, high and low (possibly) even worse. You have gifts which will be sorely needed by the world when it comes to its senses. You need this time in further study to develop your gifts, not throw them away on a muddy field of slaughter. How can I permit it? Please do not speak of the War!"

"Sir, I cannot think of anything but the War. The days pass, the news from France grows worse. These gifts you speak of I can use after I have done my bit. You cannot deny me that, sir. You must not. How could I possibly look at myself in the shaving mirror. You speak so much about if I stay at home, watch others go and stick to books!"

"Young man, if it were not for the regard in which I hold your parents I would find your impertinence beyond the pale. When you have thought this through you will know that I am, on this occasion and perhaps for once, right and you will come to see it that way."

"Sir, you once told me that a man of parts and talents bestowed by heaven must look into his own heart and make up his mind according-ly. The world may turn one way and the individual must decide which way he turns. I am resolved. I want to fly. I need to fly. I am needed to fly, as begging your pardon you know only too well as I see you daily reading the dispatches from the front. I would like to go with your blessing, or at least your acquiescence. The kind permission you gave for me to pursue this extra passion of mine has proved I am capable beyond doubt. With your permission I stand a chance of a commission and at least to lead with the compassion, grace and understanding of men's hearts that you have tried to instil. Without it, the struggle will be harder, but I am determined."

This most forbearing of men tried once more: "I called you up here to give you the good news that my old College tutor was visiting next week and we could take tea with him and take his temperature for entrance papers this Summer. Instead, you come here on the Wings of Mars preaching the manly virtues of joining the carnage across the

Channel. No, I tell you!"

"Sir, it is to be the harder route then. So be it. The recruiting office queue awaits. I am booked for the 8 at the heads-of-river and the school tennis against Radley. I will fulfil these obligations, as you have taught me, and then will take my leave. I had hoped for your blessing. I must endure, and prevail, without.... good evening Sir."

I left the twilight-bathed study in youthful indignation and not a little hot of temper. On reaching the ground and out into the Quad, I looked back up to this wholly good man's study window. He looked as though he had received bad news of the worst kind. I knew I had ended his dreams for me, in one heated conversation.

The heads-of-river regatta proved well, and I played my best tennis singles match of my entire school career, followed by a doubles match of equally historic character. The weekend ahead lay heavy as I knew I must tell my parents of my intent. The post was waiting on my return. An envelope in the inimitable hand of JM Robertson-Rhodes, marked for my attention – Master JAK Tilyard Esq. My mother's enquiring eyes implored more information, but she knew better than to ask, and busied herself with the prospect of the weekend guests my father was bringing home from London via Twyford rail station. I opened the envelope, it contained another marked: To Whom It May Concern, His Majesty's Armed Forces, Private and Confidential. I can recall the content of that letter word for word across these decades:

Dear Tilyard

I do not approve of your intentions but as far as a Master can respect the resolve of his pupil, I do extend that to you. I believe that you are in grave error endorsing by your actions the supreme folly of our national and international leaders in the matter of this repugnant War. I feel the decades ahead will be marked irrevocably by it and bring yet more disaster. However, in as much as this passion of yours for flying was helped and facilitated by my unwitting hand, I must bear the responsibility for my part in its creation and amplification. The road ahead, foolhardy and vainglorious that I believe with all my aging heart to be, will be infinitely harder if you left us to join the 'ranks'. The forces will profit, in my view undeservedly but undoubtedly from your natural leadership skills. It is only the smallest comfort that with those skills deployed in their favour, those serving with you may live a little longer. As might you. The enclosed I leave to your discretion, although I do believe that one of the lessons, we hope to pass on at this establishment is that a gentleman does not read correspondence intended for another. Do with it as you wish.

I understand the Victor Ladaurum cup is yours by right and acclamation. I have left it for collection in the Bursar's office, along with your leaver's tie.

I would wish that God went with you, if I considered you might give Him a second thought. I do not, for I cannot. I pray for your parents. Please give them my regards and be sure to let them know I will make sure a cheque in remittance of next term's school fees is returned to them. They face enough as it is without the financial loss of a son not being educated.

I am, remain and will always be your Headmaster. In shade and sun, joy, and sorrow. I will not press you to take a final leave of me, your fellows or your school. I will, however, ask of you that you remember what we tried to instil as adherents to our Founder's philosophy. One day non-violence will rule the heart of man. I had such high hopes it would start with you and your generation. I am forced to think, however, not yet and it lays heavy on my soul.

Yours,

JM Robertson-Rhodes

Headmaster, Hopkins School. Berkshire

I stood in the hallway of my family home and cried the tears of a boy who realised he had broken with a respected older man. It was as if I held in my hands a letter detailing the death of much-loved relation or close family friend. In some ways it was a kind of death, for me and for that extraordinary man who had nurtured, encouraged and supported me and now could not bear the thought of further association, lest the emotional burden be too much. Could he, would he ever forgive me, and how in the years ahead I longed for that forgiveness!

With what should have been a fillip in my cap but felt like a chain on my soul. I prepared my mother for the news that I had, by dint of that letter, now left school and was preparing to join up. She took the news with her customary elan, elegance and grace and was reassured that leaving school was with the acquiescence, if not the blessing of the headmaster, whom she if such a woman was capable of such an emotion, revered. I pointed out that my plan may still come to naught, with me a private in the Catering Corps, depending on the letter of reference from Mr. Robertson-Rhodes. That is a mystery which would reveal itself in due course, but meanwhile a weekend had to be arranged.

Father arrived back from his Henley office which he used when not working from his study at the house or in London meetings with past, ongoing, or potential clients. He could not afford a motor car, which was just becoming available to those not in the wealthy strata, but as ever was his custom, his nature and his talent, he knew people who in turn knew people who could give access to such unobtainable prizes. A trip to Paris on the boat train with a few nights at the Crillon, dinner at the Eiffel Tower and a night at the opera? One of his clients would provide –"Ah, a client of mine knows a chap who won first prize in a raffle, can't go himself so thought we could make use of them." Or a day at the races: "deuced thing, turns out that my client's brother-in-law breeds racehorses at Ascot and has couple of tickets for the royal enclosure – good job he's also got a morning suit in my size, eh?" When Father appeared with a car the size of the outhouse, bearing the unmistakable flying lady denoting the mark of a Rolls-Royce his words were: "never guess what? A client of mine has had a bit of a run-in with his debtors, needs us to make sure this doesn't go astray – says drive it around as much as you like."

Somehow, we, and all in his life, were always taken away by his enthusiasm, energy, charm and sheer force of personality. We did not make too many forays into the whys and wherefores of his advisory business or these 'clients'. Suffice it to say when they appeared he became even more animated. They brought with them more bounty: food, wine, hampers, books, tickets to this exhibition and that first night. Only once did I happen upon money in the form of cash or cheques changing hands, and that involved a be whiskered, jovial man sitting in Father's study with a pen and cheque book in hand, the destination of the largesse being handed very pointedly yet very elegantly into mother's safekeeping. These cheques, of whose provenance we never knew, were banked monthly by Mother personally at Twyford. Many decades later I discovered quite by chance that the man who wrote those cheques had himself been saved from certain ruin by dint of some timely intervention of Father's which salvaged his reputation and allowed him to build the fortune he dipped into to help upkeep the foundation of his saviour – us.

CHAPTER THREE

The house party that spring of 1918 was, paradoxically in recollection the gayest – in the old-fashioned sense of the word – that I can remember of those years which a fellow veteran of the Front, a future Prime Minister and publisher, would one day call, "those halcyon days of my youth." The rather somnolent Liberal government of HH Asquith had given way to the forceful Liberal administration of the man known to those that knew him as the Welsh wizard, David Lloyd George. The war was to be prosecuted more vigorously and policy pushed more stridently. Politicians came for a weekend to breathe the country air and plan the next moves. Newspaper columnists and correspondents gathered to discuss what was going on at the heart of government and what conspiracies were being laid behind the door at No 10 Downing Street. Writers came for plots to novels, playwrights to advance their scripts and actors not conscripted to lobby for work: a couple of sculptors and an artist of the new pointillist school I seem to remember came and went, stayed, and lingered, many with glasses and cocktail sticks in hand. I was on the verge of leaving the embrace of a world I had always known, of happy family and fulfilled as a schoolboy can be, for the uncertainty of volunteering for a cause I had taken on in order to satisfy a yearning for flight. The cause was vaguely King and Country, but the passion was for the air. I had no clue of what lay before me except the confidence of youth, a plausible manner, a speaking voice not to be ashamed of, a height which got me noticed if nothing else. In short, what others have called charisma, a term I did not then, and do not now, employ as self-description. The two words which summed up my headmaster's ideals, as perhaps the greatest man I ever knew, which he made it his life's mission to pass on, that denotes a real gentleman in its original Shakespearian meaning was, and remains, *self last*.

On that last weekend of my old life, and as I record these thoughts, could I honestly say that I had lived up to that ideal, or would ever hope to?

The weekend passed in a galore of people, talk, discussion, controversy, cigarettes and cigars, the clink of glass and the fizz of tonic on ice, a little dancing and not a little flirting, a hint of rumpled bedclothes in country hotels. In short, what I was later to come to know and recognise as the English 'middles to uppers' at play. I observed but was not amongst, stood back whilst amidst, knowing that 'we' were in our own 'class,' played by our own rules, whilst observing the proprieties. I came to learn soon enough that I danced to a different tune, the legacy of my family and a blessed existence hitherto, having found only encouragement at school and support at home. I was perhaps a little over-confident but at least I was not insecure. Which, as things transpired, was just as well.

Monday morning came bright and cold, and I set out for Henley, the local office of recruitment. As ever, Father was 'going in that direction' and could give me a lift courtesy of a friend's car he had purloined to take it to be serviced out of town by a 'chap who is a whizz with the mechanics.' We set off, almost identically dressed. When I put my school uniform aside, I decided that the only way I could emulate my father, as much an elder brother as a figure of authority, was in his manner of dress. He had a kind of uniform which he made his own and I followed: the centrepiece was the blue blazer with brass buttons, double breasted; the trousers were corduroy, invariably brown but occasionally red or blue. The shoes always brown brogues. The stand-out feature, remarked upon throughout the time I knew him, was the fact that he never wore a stiff shirt or collar, except when in borrowed clothes at the races or other sporting event. Most days of his life, my father wore a rollneck garment, which was to become known as the 'polar neck' when popularized by Arctic explorers, beneath his blazer, overlaid by a light V-neck sweater in winter and spring. No-one ever asked 'old Tilyard' why he sported such clothing, it was as known a fact as Victoria had been followed by Edward as monarch and the Fridays-to-Mondays of old were to be re-christened 'weekends'. In short, once accepted it became unremarkable amongst those who knew. It was one of the signal moments of my life with the enigma that was my father to come down from the bedroom when called to the car on that fateful Monday morning, only eighteen years into the new century, adorned in my version of his daily wear. Indeed, a carbon copy. He smiled that infectious grin which had dazzled debutantes and businessmen alike, said, "what a picture of sartorial elegance you look, my boy. Let's go in search of what adventure can be found in Henley-on-Thames this lovely morn." Thus, I was his in spirit for life.

The redbrick building overlooking the Thames which served as the outpost for the War Office in this part of the world, was full of bustle and mayhem. Father dropped me outside it and I alighted from the car to curious looks and a cheery wave from my high-spirited parent. Behind the Doric columns was a cavernous entrance way with rows of men in queues in front of two desks marked Army and Navy. No Air Force. I flagged down a likely-looking chap in uniform and asked where I should go for flying recruitment.

"O, one of the fly-boys are you? 'Fraid to say the word is that quota has been filled this month, no more places. Besides, you'll have to get past Colonel Bristow, who'll eat squibs like you for breakfast. Best join the army queue and forget all about the air."

Determined not to be put off at first blush, and not recognising the derogatory use of old-line public-school slang 'squib,' I persisted.

"Still, begging your pardon, I should like to try. Where may I find the Colonel?"

"Glutton for punishment you are. Up the stairs, along the corridor and first door on the right. Do not tell me I didn't warn you and do not tell the Colonel, I sent you. You'll be back here in quick smart time, begging for the nearest trench, mark my words..."

With that cheery brutishness he went on his way, and I made mine upstairs as directed. I came across the door, as he had directed, and knocked. The meeting which was to change the direction of my life more profoundly than any other as it started the chain of events which has led me, across a century, to this hour, started with a deep bark "Come!"

I entered a large, high-ceilinged room which had at one end a long table, in the centre of which sat the man in possession of that commanding basso-profundo. He had a large head and a profusion of dark glistening hair, greying at the temples. A large moustache, popular with military men known as a handlebar sat upon his upper lip as if it were a lovingly maintained suburban privet hedge. He beckoned me further into the room with another barked command-come-question:

"Well, what is it? Any damned fool knows that I am not seeing any more applicants today as the quota is filled! Are you a damned fool, or just dressed as one?"

I ignored the remark about my attire, knowing that the years would bring a host of similar remarks and ventured again:

"Please, if you would sir, I come with a letter from my old headmaster and am very keen to fly."

At this news the Colonel went a shade of puce as though steam would burst from his ears at any moment: "Have you indeed? A letter, from your headmaster no less. Have you *any idea* how many letters I have read from schoolmasters? Do you? Have you any idea how many people have developed the notion in their tiny minds that flying is 'quite the thing to do.' We are fighting a War of National Survival and they send me young prigs in blazers with letters!"

By this point, the imagined steam had not appeared, and the apparent rage subsided. "Get over here, let me look at you. Sit down boy, shut up and answer some questions. Tall bugger aren't you. So, where were you at school and are you of age or just trying to get past the age barrier under the wire?"

I told him I was at school near Reading at a place called Hopkins School, which was met with a look of blank indifference.

"So, not even a proper public school. That won't help." I may have looked crestfallen but continued undaunted. "Sir, I have left school early. I got my leaving certificate a year early so being a scholar they allowed me to take flying lessons and..."

The Colonel's colour turned another shade of red: "What damned rubbish are you spouting, boy! Where on God's green-filled earth did you have flying lessons? Do not lie to me boy or I shall have you sent to the catering corps on fatigues for the duration of this war and the next!"

I explained to the Colonel that due to my advanced learning I was allowed to have some free time during the school week and I managed to persuade a friend of my father to take me up in a pre-war machine.

"My God, boy, if I was your headmaster, I would have punished you twice daily for such impertinence. Be that as it may, it shows initiative. Well, don't just sit there, you blazered ninny, give me the letter!"

At this point even I, frightened as I was, had detected a softening in the Colonel's tone if not volume. I handed over the letter. I had not steamed open the letter, however much it tempted me. It was the moment of truth. I could be sunk for ever or lifted high. The Colonel began to read, and the atmospheric temperature in the room eased. He looked at me, looked back at the letter, looked at me again. "I take it, boy that you have not read this letter?"

"No sir, I considered steaming it open, but my mother threatened me with the walloping of my life if I even touched it before I brought it here."

The Colonel smiled. "Very wise woman your mother, right approach". "Tilyard, Tilyard. Read a book before the war by a VE Tilyard, some account of women chaining themselves to railings in search of the vote – that's the spirit I thought, though damned rum thing to give it to them, still."

"Yes sir, the writer of that book is my mother…".

"Good lord, Tilyard, well done her – at least you have a damned fine woman as a mother to recommend you – entirely undeserved good fortune…"

The Colonel was about to resume reading, when another thought penetrated the great domed head which made the moustache bristle. "Tilyard, there's a theatrical Johnny whom my wife, the memsahib, knows from her group, only met him once – not a habitué of the theatre myself – has an extraordinary sense of dress – blazer and cords to the dress circle…"

The Colonel stopped in mid-sentence and contemplated the vision before him, the vision that was me. "I say, Tilyard, at a guess he must be…"

"Yes sir, not at all afraid to claim him as my father, sir…"

The Colonel grunted. The reading continued. "Tilyard, I am now going to take extraordinary measures which the extraordinary situation demands of me. I am going to reveal to you, for your ears only, the spirit of the letter before me. Not exactly the contents, written from one gentleman to another, sight unseen and person unknown. If you reveal what you have heard in this room to a living soul whilst the participants live, I will have you cashiered before you can say 'Sop with Camel.' Do you understand?" I nodded and waited. "You sir, are perhaps the luckiest young man breathing on His Majesty's soil today. Undeserving as you are the supreme gentleman who has written this, refers to you as 'the finest and most abundantly gifted boy I have ever taught in 40 years of school-mastering'. He continues, "his intellectual, sporting and personal qualities are beyond his years and leadership potential is undisputed. In all frankness, the forces of his Majesty would be fortunate to have him amongst their number."

I stared transfixed and on the verge of the breakdown of tears when the Colonel continued his torrent, as if he had not noticed my stupefaction. "The clincher is the last paragraph which I hesitate to read aloud but confirms the greatness of this man's soul and thus the truth of what he says, gilded as the praise and the prose maybe: 'I may add the final accomplishment to his roster which should recommend him to whomsoever reads this – he has become accustomed to flying machines, can drive and knows one of end of a camera from another. I gave him leave, when many others would have denied him on pain of expulsion if caught in flagrant breach of rules. I cannot deny I helped facilitate this turn of events, although I was purblind and self-deluding in the matter. I do this with a heavy heart for I believe with every fibre of my being that this War is a catastrophe from which we may never fully recover and into which I wholeheartedly wish we had not entered."

I sat benumbed, tears running. For a man who I loved and respected, and at the last had begun to doubt. Colonel gave me a moment to compose myself and said in a tone of voice almost gentle by comparison: "well you may shed tears, boy. Your very accomplishments are an obvious source of pride and pain to a man who clearly saw you as a scholar and not a warrior. You have wronged him sir, but he sends via you a gift I cannot ignore. I am in need of warriors and turn your talent to the war-making arts. Then, you can be fashioned for peace if you still live. I ask you once, once only and do not answer me lightly boy or so help me God...."

We sat for the next minute in silence. The offer had been made and accepted, the business concluded. I was now under military discipline for all intents and purposes, save for the technicality of wearing a uniform. The Colonel stood to signal the end of the interview. "Tilyard, I will give you three days, on account of your mother, to arrange your affairs. Be at Reading station at 9.30am sharp on Friday morning for entrainment to Paddington and thence training camp. I need not remind you that you are soon to be the property of the British Armed Forces, body and quite possibly soul. Now leave, fast, before I change my mind. I have stretched a point, sir. Do not look at me in pathetic gratitude. I am not proud of what I have done this day. A book-learned boy with talent to share is about to learn to kill or be killed. Fact is we need men, and fast. One more thing Tilyard, take notice and make notes. Go."

I got up to leave, and by some odd compulsion, I saluted the Colonel. He gave a curt nod and resumed his seat to busy himself with the mountain of paper on his desk. I wandered back the way I had come into this powerful man's presence.

I passed through the lobby of the recruitment building, now thronged with more bodies lining up at the desks. I walked out into the Spring sunshine, and contemplated how I was going to return home. Father chose that moment to arrive in his borrowed car as if prompted by some cosmic hand, having sought and found his day's adventure in Henley, and off he went back over the river into Berkshire and the direction of home. I began to recount my story, but Father was more preoccupied with his story of the day about a chum he had bumped into, whom he had not seen since the opening night of Oscar Wilde's final play *The Importance of Being Earnest*, over 20 years previously.

"Deuced thing, he hasn't changed a bit, old Morley, just the odd grey hair. We had a natter about this and that, he very generously squared us a round, mentioned he had a son 'at the Front', asked after your mother. Odd thing was he didn't want to talk business or events of the moment, left rather abruptly now I think of it. Still stirred a memory of when my client Oscar was the talk of the town..."

Father, as was his habit and some would say his great virtue, had once again retrieved a happy thought from a well of potential despond and off we were once more on an even keel. Mother would have to be the repository of my tale to be told.

The days passed in a helter-skelter, almost blurred headlong rush of packing, talking, walking, more talking and more walking as if we needed to say everything possible in case it would be long before we got the next chance. Dawn came bright on the appointed day, and I made my way, with Father's good offices via the motor car to Reading station. There at the ticket end of the barrier stood the interviewing Colonel, Bristow. He met me with a cheery wave and beckoned me to him. All previous signs of exasperation, animosity, anger, or antipathy had evaporated. He was a picture of bonhomie and good humour, domed head glistening:

'Ah, Tilyard. Got here as instructed. How is your esteemed Mama? Well done, splendid. Now, Tilyard, there has been something of a change of plan. A little irregular but wartime and all that. You are going direct to the School of Photography in Hampshire where intensive photographic training will begin, alongside familiarisation with aircraft, weapons and other matters.

"But sir, I thought I was going for pilot training...."

"Tilyard, as soon as you learn that you are now the property of His Majesty, the better. Don't 'but sir' me, I have much sympathy for your old Head – saintly in his forbearance he must have been. Let me introduce you to a few realities, Tilyard. I am under orders; you are under orders. There is a chain of command. I have spent the last few days in communications with persons who seem to think that you are to be treated differently than the run of the mill aspiring officer to be. I have no idea why. If you are wise, and know what is good for you, you will contain yourself to obeying orders with good grace. Does the phrase, 'ours not to reason why...' have any resonance?"

"Tennyson, sir. Was that not before the light brigade charged into the mouths of the Russian guns at Balaklava, sir?"

"Tilyard, don't be a prig, don't show off and do not attempt to be clever with me or by God, I'll have you dropped into no-man's land without the benefit of a compass. Be as all that may, my orders are to put you on the train to Farnborough and to give you this. Do not open it until you are on the train and moving. Do you understand? A simple 'yes sir' will suffice."

He handed me a large, unmarked official-looking buff envelope. From somewhere deep within, unbidden and unforced, I felt a tingling sensation I could not explain.

"Thank you sir."

We walked in silence to the platform where the Farnborough train stood waiting, men, and women in uniform and out, carrying kit bags and other gear, bustling about. We stopped. This large, outwardly fearsome, brusque yet essentially kind man, took some tickets from his tunic pocket and handed them to me. "Nearly forgot. Won't get very far without these. Well, Tilyard, goodbye and good luck. And for the Almighty's sake if not for your own, pay attention!"

He turned to go, and for some unfathomable reason, possibly because I had a penchant then and have it still, you may have noticed, for the last word but also perhaps because I had come to know and have affection for this man who seemed to have a hand in my affairs so directly.

"Sir! Thank you again, sir. I won't let you or Mr. Rhodes-Roberston down, sir."

"I didn't think you would, Tilyard, didn't think you would. Now get on that train!"

And then he was gone through the steam and smoke of the train station. I boarded the train – first class tickets indeed – found a seat and made myself comfortable. By now I was bursting to open the envelope. I waited until the train pulled out of the station and unsealed the large, buff envelope. It contained a special wartime commission, signed by Colonel Bristow. He had given me a gift beyond price, his trust. The enclosed note, which I read in shock: "Tilyard, in order to be designated a temporary gentleman and thus eligible for a commission, it would have been most convenient if you had had the benefit of a Cadet Force at school. As your saintly head, in his wisdom, decided against such an organisation, I have gazetted you such anyway. Temporary or not to the Army, you shall live by those principles all the days of your life if you are to honour your education, your family, and my, possibly wayward, faith in you."

It read:

"George, by the Grace of God, of the United Kingdom of Great Britain and Ireland, and of the British Dominions beyond the Seas, King, Defender of the Faith, Emperor of India Etc."

To our Trusty and well-beloved Jeremy Anthony Kenvin Tilyard. Greetings.

We are reposing especial Trust and Confidence in your Loyalty, Courage and good Conduct, do by these Presents Constitute and Appoint you to be an Officer in Our Special Reserve of Officers. You are therefore carefully and diligently to discharge your Duty as such in the Rank of 2nd Lieutenant or in such higher Rank as We may from time-to-time hereafter be pleased to promote or appoint you to....,

.... Given at Our Court at Saint James's, this day of X 1918, in the 8th Year of Our Reign. By His Majesty's Command.... Signed on his behalf, Colonel CRF Bristow, Intelligence Corps.

I was, apparently, a temporary gentleman and had a commission to prove it! The train made its way down to Farnborough through the countryside of southern England, and I had time to contemplate the speed of events which had transplanted me from schoolboy to neophyte commissioned officer in a matter of weeks. Why had I been singled out for such rapid preferment?

CHAPTER FOUR

I was met at the station by a burly non-commissioned officer dressed in a battle-tunic standing at the other end of the platform, bearing a placard with the name Tilyard emblazoned on it. He regarded me with what seemed like a mixture of minor incredulity and dismissiveness: "are you the young personage I have been sent to retrieve and bring back to base?" "Ah, I am, yes er...Sergeant." "Come along then, quick as you can...until further notice I shall address as you as young sir and you me as Sergeant Pike, do we understand each other? All this is most irregular, most irregular...."

He led me across the station concourse to a waiting vehicle, a covered truck with a canopy and a large red cross painted on two sides. It was, as it looked, an ambulance. Sergeant Pike gave me a look which discouraged further questions and I climbed into the passenger seat, he to the drivers. We drove in silence for a while until, in a burst of what I came to know as Sergeant Pike's natural good humour gushing forth in a torrent of questions and comments: "So, young sir, very tall aren't you? Do you think you'll fit into the flying machines? Not long left school, have you? Have you got any idea about what all this is about? All I can tell you is that its got the CO in a right bait, messages from higher authority to receive a wet-behind-the ears barely-out-of-school boy for special training. Not even arrived and you have made yourself a bone of contention, and no mistake. Boys arriving on trains out of the blue, without a by-your-leave and old Pike here sent to retrieve said passenger.... most troublesome I must say...."

It seemed to me that this stream of talk did not need an answer, and whatever imprecations I had committed had been forgiven. At any rate, there was no appropriate point to interject in the one-way conversation Sergeant Pike was having with himself and the world at large, so I sat and smiled, nodded my assent from time to time and shook my head at other moments. We journeyed along Hampshire roads on this Spring Day in 1918 as if the war was indeed a long, long, way a-winding as one of the popular songs had it. The man sitting next to me was certainly the personification of those who sang another popular soldier's song of the time - *Pack Up Your Troubles in Your old Kit Bag and Smile, Smile, Smile.* Reasoning why was somewhere in the mix.

A little while and a few further conversational barrages later and we arrived at our destination, the Photography school. Pike indicated that I should make my arrival known, "quick smart as the CO, Colonel Kennard, does not like being kept waiting, particularly by young shavers like you..." In the meantime, he would have care and control of my bag. I was, indeed, in a new world.

I was ushered into his office and saw immediately that my arrival was not to be heralded with trumpets and acclamation. For a start, the Commanding Officer (CO) was as tall as I so that in-built advantage of height which was to often prove a considerable one as the years advanced, was not a winning factor in this case. He looked me over rather disapprovingly, as if to say, "now listen, I'm normally the tall one round here."

"Look here, whoever you are..."

"Tilyard sir.."

"I have a war to win and do not appreciate having young men, fresh out of school, being foisted upon me with late-night telephone calls from persons in higher authority. I have no idea who you think you are but do not imagine for one moment you can breeze in here, without a bye your leave and expect the red-carpet treatment just because you may have connections and know people."

These last few words he spat out as if expelling a nasty piece of phlegm from the back of his throat.

"But, sir, I don't know what you can mean. I am as much surprised as you that I find myself here. All I know is that Colonel Bristow sent me down here days after our first meeting at the recruitment hall in Henley, with a commission and instructions to pay attention..."

"Do not talk to me about Colonel Bristow. That confounded intriguer has torn up the Kings Regulations and no mistake. However, I am given to understand that you are familiar with aircraft. God knows how, and that you know something of photography. That is the essence of what we are about here, Tilyard. Fighting the aerial reconnaissance, observation, and photography war..."

I handed Colonel Kennard the papers I had been nursing in my blazer pocket and he unfurled his long legs from under the chair and crossed them in a movement I knew intimately as it was my own as a fellow creature of height, and suddenly softened the hard edge to his tone. "Look, Tilyard, needs must. I need photographer observer-pilots who can act as intelligence officers. I don't suppose I should be choosy as to where I get them. Seeing as you are here, with papers to say you are a temporary gentleman if not quite an officer, and judging from your attire you look more artist than warrior, I suppose we should make a fist of it. Our irregular Colonel instructed you to pay attention, did he? Well, we must make sure you do not disappoint..."

With that the interview was over. I got up to leave: "I don't suppose, young Tilyard, you have had time to organise more suitable clothing? Of course not. This irregularity is catching but so as to fit in and not go round the place looking like a refugee from the artists' colony, you can borrow a spare tunic of mine pro tem. Not very many of us with our measurements. I gather you have made the acquaintance of Pike. He'll see to it. Expect you are hungry. Busy day and all that. Go. Before I change my mind, have you reduced to the ranks and shipped out...."

I left the man who was to be the third in the triumvirate of mentors shaking his head in frustrated wonder at the turn of events that had brought me into his ken and keeping.

And so it was that I kept in his ken and in his keeping, and never was there a stronger advocate for my well-being nor better defender of my safe passage than he. I learnt in those weeks and months under the Colonel Kennard's tutelage all the arts of leadership that the combined advocacy of my sainted headmaster and Colonel Bristow had proclaimed I was suited for. In those months with him as my constant guide I learnt the nuts and bolts of aerial photography, to read a map and the contours of the land, to extract every nugget and penny piece of information from images taken from the air to better guide the troops on the ground. I was exposed for the first time to the challenges of decision-making, of strategizing and the wisdom of tactics. I learnt the art and science of small-arms weaponry and was introduced to the pistol. I was allowed to choose from an array of such arms, and for reasons that seemed lost in the mists of those far-off times but probably to be 'different', if not provocative, I chose a German design, the Walther. I never stopped reading – books, pamphlets, newspapers, classic texts, histories, plays and poems for my better understanding of human nature. I fiddled with radio-telegraphic machines and was shown the latest hand-held camera and told that the first, second, third rule of photography was 'always to have the camera with you'. It was my finishing school, my university, staff college, all in one. It was the beginning of one and the end of another sort of education and the opening of my life. I had the impression, for whence and where I do not know, that I had been chosen, selected, marked out, even vouchsafed for something. Other young, keen, clear-eyed men came and went on courses, stayed short times and left – "for the Front" said Sergeant Pike with great celerity and certainty. The other curiosity was that I flew very seldom. When I queried the Colonel about this lack of flying hours to get my 'wings' he smiled enigmatically and said, "Ah, young Tilyard, all in time, all in time – fences must not be rushed, nor rapids entered too hastily.".

One day I summoned up the courage to have it out with the Colonel in his office as to what was going on. I knocked on the door, was bidden enter and with a friendly, "Ah, Tilyard, my boy, come in – how may I be of assistance? Take the weight off and the height down, what?" This was the Colonel's customary hearty greeting and signal about our mutual predicament of height and meant kindly. That day I was in no mood for flummery and off-puts.

I folded into the chair. "Now look here sir, I am a bit frustrated and puzzled. I have been here some months now, have learnt a great deal, am fighting fit, but have had little time in the air, and received no orders of any kind. May I ask what is really going on, begging your pardon and all that, sir?"

The Colonel smiled his most expansive, avuncular smile, the most charming of those in his armoury of gestures, folded his hands on his desk and explained: "Well, Tilyard, I could take that as insubordination of the highest magnitude and put you on cold showers, bread and water and daily runs for your effrontery, but it may come as mild relief that I will refrain from such action. In this man's Royal Flying Corps and now newly created Royal Air Force mark you, it may not have escaped your notice that we are all under orders. I am no exception. Your arrival here, unorthodox as it was, and subsistence and sustenance here, is the subject of orders which may have not escaped your notice, I am in the business of following. You obviously were educated at an unconventional establishment, or this kind of questioning authority would have been knocked out of you. Still and all, as my Irish mother used to say, you are who you are and no mistake. The fact is, Tilyard, my order is that you are to remain here following the lines you have been until my orders change. When they do, you shall be the first to know but the good Lord knows why I put up with it.

Now, as for flying I happen to know that a personage of great renown among us flying chappies is visiting here soon and he wants a dekko of our bit of country from the air. I may, and I say, *may*, let you go up with him. Must say I sympathise with wanting to get into the air. Between the letter and the spirit of the standing instructions that govern your existence here, I daresay we could stretch a point, Tilyard. On this occasion. Be advised, this is not a new regime. It is my discretion. Now before I change my mind, get out young man! Fast!"

I was dismissed. I raised my self back to my full height, gave the most regulation salute a junior could give his commanding officer, said 'Sir!" in the most conventional manner and turned to leave. At the door, the Colonel called again "Tilyard". I turned, 'sir?' "Sarcasm does not become an officer; it is as you know the lowest form of wit and I would not deploy it. It behoves you ill. Go."

He half-smiled and I knew we were back on even terms. For he had indeed become the third in the triumvirate of men who I would not have wanted to think ill of me, or do anything to disappoint, for all the world. Men who had touched me in ways I did not know were possible until that moment. Men who had and were shaping me and would be the great influences on my life, save of course for the women. The man who had schooled me, the man who had commissioned me and the man who was training me. I realised at that moment that I wanted to live up to their expectation of me, with all my heart. At that moment, in that place, all-too fleetingly, I had a clear-eyed view of that dysfunctional organ known as the heart and its place in the predicament known as life and how it governs that condition referred to as human. I loved these men, and I owed them my allegiance, my unswerving loyalty and my faith and trust, whatever lay in the future.

CHAPTER FIVE

C ame the day when the personage arrived in our corner of England. He arrived with the minimum of fuss, having been collected from the station, as I had been by the inevitable and always-pre-
sent, Sergeant Pike. The man who emerged from the military vehicle
was clearly familiar with the Pike Approach, for he wore on his face
an expression of half-exasperation and half-affectionate indulgence
that only a close encounter with Pike could bring forth. I wondered
what mode of address had been directed towards this very senior
officer. His badged rank was Colonel but in the new dispensation of
rankings in the new force of air, these were to change. Sergeant Pike's
solution to the potential procedural, and social, embarrassment was
as original as the owner of the fertile mind who had dreamt it up. I
was soon informed. As welcoming committee it played out in front
of me as if committed to the moving image camera: Pike opened the
door for his passenger who emerged from the cab, with a "Here we
are Wing-Colonel Command, Sir, your destination and look, with
young Tilyard to put out the welcome mat." Tall, though not quite
my height, a patrician but kindly air masked by a forbearing man-

ner. "Thank you, Sergeant Pike. I shall practise those songs, much obliged." I am sure I heard a faint whistle of a popular tune play on his lips, one which was to become famous throughout the world down through the ages, penned by an Anglo-Welshman, Ivor Novello, known of course to my father - Keep *The Home Fires Burning*. Pike took possession of this senior officer's bag with a proprietary air that would brook no opposition, even if it had belonged to His Majesty himself. The visitor gave up the unequal struggle, knowing when to beat a tactical retreat, and turned a pair of piercing cobalt blue eyes upon me.

"Ah, the welcoming committee. Am I much mistaken or have I come into a land of giants in this corner of England's green and pleasant? Now look here, young man, I am most always one of the tallest people in encounters, but I suppose it had to happen sometime – the meeting of the yet taller. After Sergeant Pike, here, I am firmly of the view that just about anything is possible. Lead on Macduff!"

His open aspect, his frankness of manner, the engaging style had sparked in me another tingle of excitement, as inexplicable as it was unexpected. I offered a reply in something of the same jaunty tone: "Well, sir, I see you have made the acquaintance of Sergeant Pike. A word to the wise, Sir, the CO is well, how to put this, quite as tall as I. Just so you know..."

"By the Lord that looks after all, what is it about flying machines and gigantic personages? I suppose if we were meant to fly, he who created us would have given us wings, and yet, and yet..."

I knocked on Colonel Kennard's door. He bade us enter. We did. He stood, muscular framed and Roman-headed aspect bathed in the afternoon light as it came through the blinds. He broke into a smile the width and depth of which I had not seen in this most mercurial featured of men. "Good Lord by all that is holy and not, Hugh, is that you? Is that really you?"

I had not seen the Colonel quite so animated. He almost bounded across the desk and came towards us with wide grin and hands out-stretched.

"I had no idea the personage they talked of would be you...of all people..."

"Toby! Good God! Toby Kennard! It is you. They told me nothing except I was to visit the Photography school and murmured something about information-gathering, consolidation, morale-boosting for the new service. We are Royal no less and an Air Force. No idea it would be you in command down here! The ministry life is a little uninformed."

These two senior men of arms in the air embraced as if long-lost confreres and comrades, backslapped and, in the American usage to become popular in another time, joshed. It was as if I was invisible and so I stood and watched with surprise and due regard this unlikely yet unforced and quite genuine display of brotherly affection between these two men.

As suddenly as sunshine emerging from a cloud, my existence was once more acknowledged. The Colonel said, "Ah, Tilyard, yes. Allow me to introduce Colonel Hugh Dowding, late of the RFC and now of the RAF. Man of the air and future Marshall of it!" To which Dowding responded "Would those promotions came as easily! I suppose these new ranking structures will all have to get used to. Your man Pike mangled the form of address with an air of authority that only a man who has no inferiors or superiors, just feels rank and class as a temporary predicament. Rum fellow. Very funny. That sort of running commentary he has instead of conversation. Like a warm bath or a familiar orchestral overture. Allow it to wash over you and time's swift chariot moves like lightning."

A more apt description of a man Kennard had known since the start of the war and I had come to know well these last six months, was the measure of the remarkable, protean and mercurial understanding this man had of human beings, their character and personality. He was about to shine that light of understanding on me, which was to have profound consequences.

Meanwhile, I was about to be reminded of my actual status in this roomful of senior officers. Colonel Kennard turned to me with a look that was unmistakable. "Tilyard, will you excuse us? We have much to catch up on. Time is pressing. We shall see you at dinner. As usual, 8pm sharp". And with that, I was dismissed. I nodded, saluted, this time with genuine and proper regard, and left the room.

The injunction of my old head on reading letters not addressed to oneself, also extended to listening in on conversations about oneself, particularly conducted by senior people, whether teachers, clergymen or officers. I had a strong feeling that I would feature in some way, an intuition that I yearned to back up with words on the air. There was only one way to do so. I had to contrive to listen in on some part of their exchange, but how? I made myself leave the building and, in near-despair, spotted these two officers, gentlemen and as close friends as the culture and mores of the time would allow, leave the building themselves. I had a certain knowledge, I know not where from, where they were headed and followed them at a distance, using tracking skills newly acquired at the hand of Colonel Kennard himself.

They were on their way to a bench overlooking a lake that sits in the middle of the land attached to the house where the school is based. The best time of day to sit and ruminate is around dusk, before the light goes. The late summer/early autumnal evening was perfect for such an exercise. Colonel Dowding is unaware, but Kennard knows all. They were going to have a walk, sit in companionable exchange and discuss my future. I just knew it. Full of a mixture of indignation, conceit and hutzpah that only a young man who thinks himself clever can muster, I made my plan to hide near the park bench I thought they were heading for and wait. Sure enough, in time they appeared, sat down, and were in perfect earshot of a young giant, who thought himself camouflaged but could probably be seen for miles as if he were wearing day-glow orange and whistling Tipperary. They nevertheless plunged on and the words crystal on the air:

"Now look, Toby, it may not have passed your notice that I am on a bit of a mission, and not just here for the unexpected delights of seeing you and reporting back how marvellously the school flourishes and how central it must be to the whole RAF project, as a new service and all that, though that is part of it..."

"Hugh, that much I had gathered. The Ministry needs evidence, and we shall give them it, for evidence brings money..."

"Yes, yes, Toby. There is more though. We are about to enter a crucial phase of the War, involving fighting with all that we have, which if it goes well will make the Somme and Bloody April look like a pre-war picnic on the boating lake at Regents Park, but might force the Germans to the treaty table and terms...."

"Hugh, I…"

"Toby, please don't interrupt, need to get this off the chest and then you can ask all the questions you want…"

"Now, if this, let's call it a push, is successful – planned for September/October but please do not bruit that about – we shall have thrown everything we have at the Germans, with the aid of the French and the Americans too and we shall either overcome or be plunged into many more months, possibly a year, more of attritional killing. So, it is rather important we get the planning right at least…"

They both sat, these two gentlemen-flyer-warriors, and contemplated for a short moment what the words that had been spoken meant. The possibility of peace after four long years of battle, killing, lost friends, murdered youth and wasted time that could and should have been devoted to advancing the causes of mankind, not his destruction.

"Hugh, I understand all that. It means for us here that there will be a rush of new chaps to learn the particular arts of warfare we teach. Pike will be busy fetching and carrying from the station and young JAK Tilyard, he will be…"

"He will be, indeed, Toby, he will be. He it is, partly, about whom I have come…"

" What on earth do you mean, Hugh? He has been posted here for the duration, as even he by now will have ascertained – a posting by those higher up of whose ways we cannot fathom and by whose instructs we toil and labour, remember? When he arrived here, at first, I was irritated at the thought that some gilded youth had been given a free pass of some kind. All was most irregular. Barely out of school, commissioned by Bristow of Intelligence, without a whiff of prior training but bearing recommendations as a talent to be used. So it has proved. He is a natural at anything he touches – flying, driving, shooting, map reading, photographing, report writing, languages, public speaking, lecturing. He is in short as brilliant as those that thought so said he was. He is by the way, a natural teacher. Not only do I need him here, passing all that on to the shavers that arrive and are to be dispatched to the front all too soon. It may not have escaped your notice that I have the prior claim as he has been posted here...."

"Look Toby, I sympathise I really do but you must know something which may bring some comfort. I am taking some leave from the Ministry and going back to the Front for what you might call an intelligence-gathering recce for the big plan. The Ministry wallahs, and the Prime Minister – maddening fellow but quite extraordinary - will only let me go – and it is imperative that I do – if I have an aide of some kind to arrange things, go hither and yon, help make madness sound like sweet reason and deal with fellows one would rather cashier as look at them. A liaison officer by special appointment to me, as it happens. Your chap Tilyard is that man, clear as day with arc lights attached. Would you lend me him, for a while? I could go through channels, make it look all frightfully official, especially as in their wisdom the higher ups have given me an acting Brigadier ship so as to negotiate with the French and the Americans and other Allies. All before the new ranking structures come in for this new service of ours. So, what do you say?"

Colonel Kennard began to form a riposte, but it died on his lips as he looked a mixture of crestfallen and defeated. He knew this skirmish was over before it had begun. But he also knew that his friend Hugh had dressed up an order to sound like a request and in his heart of hearts he also knew that this was the 'something' we had both been waiting for but dare not express in words for fear of bringing the moment forward. It was of course, the opportunity of a lifetime for me at the same time as robbing this soldier-flyer with poetical sensibility the company of a young man he had come to look on as a protégé.

"Hugh, or should I now call you sir, I say this is both cruel and kind. I say he is not ready. I say there will be chaps sent to me here, with gifts and youth and vigour and idealism who will never live another autumn due to the Big Plan, but with no hidden hand of protection and that they may have lived another season if they could have learnt from this extraordinary being that comes to us aged just-18 but in reality is as old as wisdom and as eternally young as Zeus. What on earth do you expect me to say? Now, go, return to London with your schemes to end the War – how many schemes in how many wars before and to come will men come up with ways to end what others started, quickly, within weeks, what has taken years? I could delay, obfuscate, put spokes in wheels of this audacious man-theft of yours. I may end in disappointment and failure but could ensure that young Tilyard is safe!"

At that point his voice dropped and there came silence and, tall as he was, he seemed to stoop on the bench, as if crushed.

"Look, Toby, I could find another aide..."

"Do not, please, sir, 'look Toby' me. We both belong too deep in this world, and you and I have known each other too long. Of course, he must go. Of course, you must have him. For you and I are the mere instruments of this hidden hand that has shaped his path. Do not look skeptical, Brigadier Dowding, you know it is true. He has been beseeching me thrice weekly for some weeks as to whether I have received any further orders. Well, now I have, and they have come in the unlikeliest of ways. You have brought an old friend to sorrow and will lift with joy that of a young man whose company I can now barely think of being without. There is a drop of ice in your veins, Hugh Dowding, and no mistake. They had to make you a Brigadier, acting or not, to come down and steal the most precious thing your oldest chum ever thought fleetingly was his for another season.

"Just promise me this, and do not reveal to Tilyard that I suggested this or requested it. Promote him to Captain before his departure, a higher rank will help him and no doubt assist you, Brigadier. And keep him close, whomsoever requests otherwise. Let him know your thinking, share your anxieties, give him challenges – people and places. Allow him to make suggestions, encourage him to keep reading, and do not worry if his manner appears insubordinate. Protect him above all from those who would bring him down because of this innate nature that the military must never quash. He is a natural independent. Nurture it, foster it, keep that flame alive. You have my blessing, though it pains me to lose him. So does he. And please, Hugh, do not pretend that this attachment will bring him back here and to me. We both know that this will not happen. Take him, with my reluctant but genuine blessing. May you have joy of him, although you, old comrade, have broken my war-weary heart."

At these words I nearly fell out of the tree I was perched in, but in retrospect I have harboured a pretty certain conviction from that time to this that the Colonel knew they had an eavesdropper and the Brigadier suspected it. It was my cue to withdraw as silently as the situation would allow and to return to the school and the Mess before my interlocutors. Anything less than total success in this enterprise would bring ruination for one nascent career, amid the embarrassment and friendship-ending for two senior officers. I ran as fast as I had ever run heretofore – for my life, for the love and respect of these good men and for the excitements of what was to come. This was indeed the something that had been long hoped-for.

Dinner in the mess was as if the previous hour did not exist in time and space. Conversation turned to the following day, and the Colonel made light, as he could when needed:

"Look, Tilyard, the Brigadier here needs a tour of our establishment and a 'dekko' of the surrounding area – what say you to being his guide and Sherpa tomorrow? What think you to getting Richtofen into the air with our visitor here along for the ride?.."

At this my heart rate rose, as Richtofen was our training aircraft, named after the German air ace, recently shot down and buried with full military honours.

At that point Brigadier Dowding's face lit up and he became quite animated: "what a first-class idea, Colonel Kennard. Must say I haven't been airside for an age, be tremendous fun. That is, young Tilyard, if you can spare the time..."

"Why, sir, of course, it would be an honour, sir."

"Now, now, young man, conserve the excitement for the morrow! If you will excuse me, it has been a long day, and a chap has to get what beauty sleep he can. So, until then, bright and early." With that Brigadier Dowding rose from the table, nodded a customary goodbye, and took his leave for quarters and bed.

Colonel Kennard gave me a long, old-fashioned look. I knew then that he knew that I knew of what passed between him and Dowding, but he gave no further indication: "he is a fine man, Tilyard, his burden very onerous, his commitment total and his integrity absolute. All virtues we can aspire to. You look after him as if here was your sainted headmaster, mother or that Bristow who interrupted my life when he sent you here. You might even have a care that he and I have been comrades, in sunshine and shadow as the old song has it, since we were boys. He is the only man in this world I fully and completely trust."

A far-away expression settled on the Colonel's face and as instantly as it appeared it left his face and he covered his evident emotion with a gruff: "well, bed for us all now. Early morning, lots to do." He rose from the table and turned to go, and then added another elliptical comment that was to later play in my mind for years to come: "Be to him as you have been to me, JAK Tilyard, that's all I ask..."

CHAPTER SIX

The Lord of the sea, land and sky could not have provided a more perfect day for flying dekko. A clear blue sky, a gentle breeze, some light cloud, visibility good. My distinguished passenger and I made the most of it. From a breakfast noted by the absence of my Commanding Officer, the first he had missed in all the days of our association. It was as if the situation had been contrived for me to spend the entire day in the company of, and perhaps being 'sized up' by Brigadier Hugh Dowding; which of course, it had. I must respond naturally without giving any hint that I knew that a game was in play. I need not have worried. Dowding was about to add his name to the growing roster of alchemical figures in my life who made the journey between the now of 'then' and the now of 'now' possible. He made things easy, natural and straightforward. Knowing that I had not flown for a long time, he offered to be the pilot for our trip up "to keep my hand in" – flying a desk has been a bit limiting of late, but there are plans a-foot, plans a-foot.

The only way I can describe that day to someone whose grandfather had not yet been born, is by way of reference to a film I saw a lifetime later, about the Danish writer Karen Blixen – *Out of Africa*. The scene when she and her friend Denis Finch-Hatton take to the skies high above the African plain. That in our own way, above the fields of Hampshire that cloudless day in 1918, we had escaped our earthly bonds and reached for the sky. Eventually, with fuel running out and time ebbing away, Brigadier Dowding, rejuvenated by his time in the air, indicated with a signal – for the noise of the cockpit precluded talk - that we were to descend. Exhilarated and exhausted in equal measure, yet ready for anything, I gave a thumbs up and we were soon enough back on terra firma. I knew then that this man was not to be lost sight of.

After the flight we were too energy-laden to return to the main building just yet so strolled about the extended grounds of the school. Dowding made his move.

"Look, Tilyard, I have a proposition for you but it is one of unusual delicacy so just listen, rather in the manner that a chap who is being addressed by a senior should, in the conventional world, which I hear has no hold on you. In other words, hear me out and say nothing..."

"Of course, sir."

"We in the senior hierarchy of what you might call the Forces of His Majesty are planning what we might call a Big Push with the objective of attacking the enemy in such overwhelming numbers that he will be forced to come to terms and thereby end the War. Now, I have obtained a certain license from those senior to me – yes, they do exist – to take some time and visit the Front, assess what may be what and report back to the Ministry the thinking of those planning this potentially war-ending move. I am being allowed what may turn out to be a little extended leave if I obtain for myself an aide, an assistant, an adjutant to assist with the practicalities – a sort of one-man general staff to facilitate ease of manoeuvre and swift observation. In other words, a chap familiar and competent in a number of areas who can be my ears, eyes, forward scout – that sort of thing. Now, the choice was either official channels and gazette a body from the staff extant or go through easier channels and attach a chap to me personally. Of course, I would quite understand if you thought that staying on here and continuing the teaching role you have is a more useful contribution to winning the War."

"Gosh, sir, well, wow, I don't know quite what to say."

"Which by all accounts is highly unusual. Look, Tilyard, I know this is something of a surprise, though I gather your tracking skills are quite well honed, but I must know your answer and soon. The thing is, was rather thinking that with you on the team we could lose no further time in getting on with it. If not, I will have to signal London, return to Whitehall, and find a willing adjutant. So, what say you? I know Colonel Kennard will feel your loss keenly, but I am borrowing you as it were, and he is squared as it were. Fine man. Never, ever, forget that."

"Sir, in the face of this, there is only one other thing to say, that is... Yes, sir, Tilyard, reporting for duty, Sir."

"That's the spirit young man. Well, now we must return to base and break the news, or confirm what he may have expected, to the Colonel."

We found Colonel Kennard at his desk, finishing a call as we entered.

He forced a jovial look: "So, how was the flight? Glorious day for a dekko, so wish I could have come with you. Has the escape plan been hatched, the lad squared, the theft official?"

"Yes sir. Gosh, sir, I don't quite know what to say..."

"Then my strong advice is, for once, to say nothing."

"When do you propose to leave, Brigadier, Sir?"

"On the morrow after phone calls and lunch."

"I suggest Tilyard here goes with you. Now, Tilyard, the Brigadier and I have a few more things to sort out. If you will excuse us...." I got up to go.

"Ah, with your leave, Toby, there is one more small detail we both should confirm. The usual practice for adjutants, unofficial or not, temporary or not, is to hold the rank of Captain. For practical, social, political, and military-efficient purposes. I propose, with your permission as this temporary officer's commanding officer, that we gazette him an acting Captain, effective immediately. Would that be in order?"

I stood there, for once, speechless. I knew Colonel Kennard had a hand in this promotion, been true to what he had spoken of that which I had overheard. It would make the new mission I was embarking on a reality.

"That, sir, is indeed in order. Charmed life our young shaver leads. Arrives here out of the blue a Lieutenant without a minute's barrack room endurance and leaves a Captain, adjutant to Dowding of the Ministry. Technically, he is in the Intelligence Corps, but we could attach him to the RAF. Tilyard, you have a damnable habit of making mavericks of us all. Now get out and start packing before the Brigadier and I have a change of heart."

"Sir, Sir, yes, both Sirs!" I saluted my best salute yet. They both smiled, threw me a knowing look instead of the inkwell on the desk, and I departed as fast as was decent out of that room where much of my fate had been decided.

My wardrobe was not extensive, so packing was not onerous. I had the blazer and trousers I had arrived at the School of Photography in, the Colonel's spare mess dress and a battledress, also belonging to the Colonel for working days. They fitted like a glove, and somehow in the last half year there had not been time to order a uniform. These were my belongings. Colonel Kennard came into my quarters and suggested I keep the mess dress and the battledress, assuring me he could spare them, and he felt sure I would at some point acquire my own. He brought a box with a few items that he thought may prove useful. The Walther pistol I had taken to at the armoury with box of ammunition; a field cap; a Sam Browne belt and a French Army field helmet.

"The word is that the former First Lord of the Admiralty, one Winston Churchill wore a helmet like this at the Front when he was sojourning there – a fellow maverick, and it somehow found its way here. Sometimes it is as well for a liaison officer, as you will be, needs a little colour about his personage. I suppose you, I, the British Army and the RAF should thank Brigadier Dowding that he has personally assigned you as Captain Tilyard to himself. As to weaponry, it is highly unlikely that you would draw in anger but if you do, at least we know it works. Fact is, Tilyard, you arrived irregularly, you will leave the same way.

Unconventional, thy name is JAK Tilyard. You have the luck of....
well, let's leave that aside. More I cannot do. I have helped you on your
way. Do not look back when you go, for I do not care to see you turned
into a pillar of salt like Lot's wife. Well, leave you to it, young giant.
Breakfast as usual."

He did not linger in my quarters; it was cramped anyway for two
sizable males. He suggested a good night's sleep and would be there
for breakfast, as was our custom. It was to be our last. The Colonel
talked of anything but the impending departure. The weather, the
new set of trainees – 'young shavers the lot of them' – set to arrive; the
trouble that Sergeant Pike was having with the new RAF rankings and
nomenclature, not quite in use yet, and the prospect of more comings
and goings. Then Colonel Kennard remembered something and leapt
up from the table, with cry of "by Jove – nearly forgot the boots!
Finish up young man. The Brigadier here is anxious to get off and Pike
equally so to get you both to the station. Meet me in the forecourt."

In the forecourt of the main building, Pike was already there with
transportation lorry and had indeed loaded my 'kit' into the back
with a "well, young man, sir, more than you arrived with!" I see the
'Colonel-Brigadier Command Wing is travelling light'. Colonel Kennard emerged from the building, his exquisite sense of timing perfect
to the last, carrying a new pair of field boots.

"Last thing, Tilyard. Some time ago I had these boots arrive as a second
pair, sent to me from, well never you mind. They have not been worn,
just polished and if I am not much mistaken, they are your size. They
may come in useful out there..."

"Sir, what can I say but thank you. For this and for everything. I...

"Tilyard, I think the Brigadier would agree when I say that when young officers effect to have nothing to say, it is best that they do not. In your case, having much, and often far too much to say, sometimes silence is golden. It may do you, and all around you a power of good if you would from time-to-time bear that in mind."

At this point Dowding smiled a smile I would come to know well in the brief time we were together: benign, indulgent, knowing. He turned to the Colonel: "Toby, is there anything else to do before the off? Your Sergeant Pike is already behind the wheel, thrumming his fingers and shaking his head at the doings of the mighty..."

Kennard looked as though he had been struck by an inspiration: "allow me this one indulgence, Sir. As there has been no official posting, no orders and no paperwork governing your arrival, sojourn and departure with a member of my staff, we had in effect a hand-over, so it cannot be said by those who may that all this was far too irregular."

"So, in my capacity as Officer Commanding the School of Photography, on this day I formally attach acting Captain JAK Tilyard to the personal staff of Brigadier Hugh Dowding, himself acting with the authority of the War Office and the Ministry of Air, as adjutant, liaison, intelligencer and all other duties that he, and he alone, may see fit." He then produced a hand-written copy of the spoken words, dated and signed, and handed it formally to me. He had evidently spent time in the reaches of the night composing it. Knowing the hidebound ways of the British military, only now changing from the ways of Waterloo and the Crimea as a result of this deadly world conflict, he had produced a 'laisser passez,' which another era would recognise as an access all areas pass.

Dowding smiled again, which turned to a little mist in the eye. He said, "duly accepted, Colonel Kennard". We three then executed between us the most formal series of salutes a household Guards officer, if he had been present at that moment, would not have seen in many a long year. At our full combined heights, Colonel Kennard and I towered above the Brigadier, himself no midget, and the English countryside. We saluted formally. He and Dowding performed the same, and the deed of hand-over was done.

Meanwhile, Pike had added shaking his head to the finger-thrumming. If he possessed a watch, he would have been looking at it and pointing to the time. The two senior officers had such a timepiece on the wrist, an innovation introduced with the developments of the War, as first worn and used by officers in front-line trenches.

"You had better get going or Pike will blow a gasket. Swift journey, safe arrival, successful mission and may God hold you both in the hollow of his hand."

With that he saluted once more and retreated back into his office. Many decades later I happened upon a lady who in those days would have been called a daily 'char,' by the coincidence of time, place and how the world turns, who had arrived to 'do' – clean. She spoke of the Colonel, 'tall as he was, standing at the window with tears running down his face, watching a lorry drive away. I didn't say a word and left him to it, thought was best.' Those tears were for me, and what he and I had shared as the fortunes of war had thrown us together. The acknowledgement of this indissoluble bond between men was put to me by the Brigadier in the course of our association, and long after when I encountered him again during the battles for survival in the skies, over 20 years later:" Toby Kennard loved you JAK Tilyard and I took you from him. Broke his heart. I hope it was worth it " .

We drove away from the school in a general state of silence, broken when Pike deemed it time to continue his stream of consciousness. Thus, with Pike's good-natured blether sounding in our ears we journeyed to the station at Farnborough, scene of my arrival those months, a half a lifetime emotionally, ago. The cosmic angels of arrangements had deemed it that there would be no awkward goodbyes or fumbled words on departure, for on our arrival at the station, a contingent of what Colonel Kennard would doubtless refer to as 'young shavers' were milling around the station concourse, as if awaiting the services of Sergeant Pike and his military vehicle.

"Ah, look, the new lot arriving. All come to learn what you did, then off to the Front. Don't look a day over 16. Mind you, young man Tilyard, sir, neither did you. They look in need of a Pike to shepherd them, so if you two gentlemen don't mind, I will leave you to it, and go about their requirements. Good lord and father of mankind, as my old mama used to say before clipping me round the ear, there is a carbon copy of you, young Sir." And sure enough, as we looked across the concourse, amongst the bodies in classic hurry up and wait mode, one figure towered above the rest, with a stance that did indeed look very familiar.

"Well, Sergeant Pike. What a turn-up, as you might say. Looks like the Colonel will have another young giant to keep him company in the clouds. Many thanks for all your close attention. Goodbye and good luck and, well, keep those home fires burning...."

Brigadier Dowding and I collected our bags and made our way into the station. I recalled the words of Colonel Kennard advising me not to look back lest I, like Lot's wife of Biblical legend, be turned into a pillar of salt. It was of course a warning not to indulge in what at that time in societal sensibility was known as unhelpful sentimentality. It was a time when matters needed to be "faced" and in a phrase which was to resonate for a couple of succeeding generations for accepting the difficult, inevitable or just the things that came out about by happenstance, whether an accidental or untimely death, an unhappy marriage, a miscarriage or a failed business venture – such things often "couldn't be helped" and spilt milk was "not for crying over." Matters of the mind had only just been officially invented by Messrs Jung and Freud and the war had brought many medical conditions and their treatments to the fore, such as "shellshock" and "nervous tension", but these were in their infancy. More readily people in authority spoke of "moral fibre" and being made of "the right stuff" or being a "good sort". In other words, a young man who had been gazetted Captain, without the sweat of the parade ground and the drudge of the barrack room, nor the boredom of the OTC, should count himself lucky to be taken up and taken on by his seniors, given scope to exercise his natural abilities and trained in as unconventional a manner as this man's armed forces could stretch to; should not indulge in 'what aboutry' and 'only ifs.'

Still and all, in Colonel Kennard's Irish mother's arresting phrase, it warmed the cockles to think that my mentor would soon be encountering another tall young man in whom he could invest his hopes, aspirations and encouragements. A lucky happening for them both. Young giant would survive the war, and the Colonel would have his heart patched up, if not quite mended.

We boarded the train bound for Paddington. Dowding had arranged for Kennard to contact the Air Ministry in London to advise them that he had been successful in finding an adjutant for his 'mission' and that he would proceed with all dispatch to France, calling in at Paris first on the British Military Mission. On the Paris train out of London, via the boat to France. In another war-time age, yet to come, an English author wrote that 'Fair Stood the Wind for France.'

It did for us as Summer gave way to the Autumn of 1918.

CHAPTER SEVEN

The City of Light was battered and bruised, no longer the epi-centre of the Belle Époque, and the surrounding landscape of Northern France and Belgium has been described, in far more descriptive terms that my mind can muster, as 'lunar.' Nothing had quite prepared me for the devastation that a war fought with the tools of the Industrial age could visit upon humanity, animals and countryside. Mud, barbed wire, trenches, churned-up farmland, men and machinery could be seen from the train as we rattled our way to the French capital city.

My first encounter with the city that was to become such a motive force in my life was set against the background of the ravages of nearly four years of war. The buildings were grey, the streets dirty, the hotels faded, the bridges across the Seine in need of a clean. The gaiety of the Belle Epoque of pre-war years had given way to 'La Guerre Mauvais.' "C'est la guerre, mon brave, mon homme gentile" was the general response to questions as to how it went and seemed to underpin the general demeanour of the city that a succeeding generation, from

Americans to students and young lovers, would take to their heart in the catchphrase of a later time, and a moving picture of the 'guerre' that was to come, 'we'll always have Paris'. That was for the future. Then, Brigadier Dowding and I were not there as boulevardiers to sample the delights of the bars, bistros, cafes and restaurants so these considerations passed us by. The plight of the lady of Paris distressed, down-at-heel and brought low was not ours to fix, so we set our compass for the British Military Mission and an encounter with another maverick that the Great Conflagration had thrown up on time and tide.

We found the Military Mission in Paris, and we also found Major-General Edward Louis Spears. He had found some fame amongst the French, and not a little approbation amongst his peers in the British Army, for his efforts at liaising with the French Army in the opening months of the war, and now providing the link between the British and French ministries of war. If he had not exactly invented the art of liaison between friendly forces, he had pioneered the modern approach to military liaison single-handedly and had, through sheer perspicacity, persistence, determination and the facility with French as a native speaker, saved the British Expeditionary Force from a catastrophic strategic blunder. In this way, in the ensuing years, he became the link between the French and the British armies, the former old enemies now locked in forced amity by the Entente Cordiale, interpreting one to the other and carrying out that vital but almost-impossible task of reading the minds of the top brass in one armed camp and communicating it to the other armed camp. He had borne the perils of this task with great bravery, skill and aplomb, and was in fact the messenger who had been shot at several times in the course of his duty on and near the front line. Edward Spears was in the business of men and their motivations, and he would demonstrate again and again in the time of our association that he had a kind of insight into the quixotic nature of the human heart as manifested by the military male, whether titans like Foch, Haig, Wilson or the harassed brigade majors and quarter masters upon whom the business of the orders of the mighty fell. Spears was to return to this mission in a later war, then in the far, unknowable distance, when he played a central role in securing the attentions, and services in a noble cause, of a then-obscure French cavalry officer called Charles De Gaulle.

Our first encounter paved the way. Another mentor-in-the-making and another link in the human chain of the extraordinary series of encounters that marked my path. We found him at his desk in the town house that served as the military-diplomatic outpost and his operational domain. We must have looked, Dowding and I, a peculiar sight – one very tall young man in borrowed tunic and a slightly shorter ascetic warrior with just a hint of a far-away look in his eyes, which was yet to become fully developed. If we did, he showed no sign. From his opening remarks, he seemed to know what we were about, without ever having been told.

"Gentlemen, come in. What brings you to this corner of the wood? Dowding of the Air, for, sir, it must be you. Who is this young giant of no fixed regimental abode? Take the weight off both, tell all and leave nothing out. My only request is that you indicate how I can help..." He had refreshments brought in and Dowding began the tale.

"Well you see Major-General Spears, we have an unusual enterprise. I have been given leave from the Ministry, taken it actually, to ascertain the facts on the ground as it were, the conditions prevailing, the situation present in advancement of what the higher-ups and the planners are beginning to call informally the Big Push. With the Americans and the Allies, it is thought we really do need to go on the offensive, break the stalemate with Fritz and, well, end the War."

The silence that followed stretched, seconds seemed like minutes. The pause to reflect, to hope, to ponder, to savour the very idea of the words, the phrase to roll around the head and then the tongue – "end the War."

Spears broke the silence with a subtle harrumph: "And where does this young giant come in?"

"Well, the Ministry would not let me go without a chaperone. To keep me from wandering off, no doubt. Tilyard here is hardly your typical idea of a maiden aunt, but I borrowed him from the School of Photography to act as my one-man staff, facilitator, smoother-over, runner-about, and, well Major-General...."

" Liaison?" Spears looked at me, smiled a broad smile, got up and shook my hand, "welcome, indeed, to my world young man. Splendid! We are a bit of a rare breed, but the powers-that-be are at last beginning to see the point. Brigadier Dowding, may I say you have started well, but you'll need all the good breaks that lady luck can bestow. Once more gentlemen...how can I help?"

"Well, Major-General. You know all there is to know about dealing with hidebound hierarchy and military intransigence, so having the imprimatur for our forays into diplomatic war-making would help a great deal. There is another consideration. Tilyard here is attached to me for the duration of our investigations. He is to all intents and purposes a Captain of Intelligence who will need a safe berth after our little show ends and the next begins. A berth with you after his attachment to me will give him safer passage in the uncertainties to come. I do not want some choleric Colonel of the line gazetting him like a playing card for the mud and the blood."

Colonel Spears fixed me with an appraising look and spoke as he had the gift of prophecy and magic insight rolled into one: "Young man, I suppose you have French? Can you, ah, drive, fly and what is your photographic eye like? They must have taught you something at that school for photographers. Not long left school proper? My guess would be a second-line establishment. Am I right? Don't worry, lad, I was passed off as not quite a gentleman because I was schooled in France. Still am in too many quarters."

I sat there, and was poked by the Brigadier to say something:

"Well, sir, thank you sir. It was a Quaker school, with no corps, but I learnt to fly and drive, as a matter of fact for my Pa had access to both from clients, and well..."

As if he had not heard my uncharacteristic nervous outburst, Spears suddenly lit up with a bonhomie smile: "Splendid, splendid. Speaks French, drives, flies and takes photographs! Tell you what. With your permission, Brigadier, when he has done with your services, come back here and I'll attach you as my adjutant/aide-de-camp, much in the same way as you are to the Brigadier here. A liaison officer's liaison officer! That will get them thinking, and spilling the beer into the beards, quite take the shine off the brylcreem, eh?" Spears had another thought. "Just to belt and brace it, if anyone asks, I'll arrange a Military Mission-Supreme War Council pass, just in case. Second thoughts I'll do it now...full name?"

"Jeremy Anthony Kenvin 'JAK' Tilyard, sir, Captain and temporary gentleman..."

Spears took out from his desk a pocket-sized document, picked up a fountain pen and created there and then, before our eyes, much in the same way Kennard had done, a laisser passez military-diplomatic pass-port, bearing the rubber-stamp of the British Military Mission and embossed with his copper-plate handwriting: 'Captain JAK Tilyard, shall have leave to go where he might, speak to whomsoever he may in the course of his duties, and requisition whatever assistance both human and material he considers in furtherance of those duties as a seconded officer of the British Military Mission. By the Grace of God and King George. Major-General Edward Louis Spears.'

Spears handed me the newly created pass, and smiled again: "That should cover it. Let me know how it goes. We will have much work to do when the Big Push is over. A war to finish. A peace to build. Liaison in excelsis. Would lend you both my car but that would push the conventions a bit too far! Am sure you can find one. Bon chance, gentlemen, Bon chance. Brigadier Dowding. Tilyard, young giant." He saluted, shook hands, resumed his seat, took up his pen once more. The meeting was over. The deed done. The next link in my chain secure, it was time to go. What we had come to France for. To make a start at the beginning of the end of nearly four long years of slaughter, with more to come before it stopped. We made our way out of Spear's office, down the balustraded staircase typical of 18th Century Chateaux style and made our way out into the early autumn sunshine of Paris.

The task now was to find transportation to the Front. In the words of the adapted soldier's parody of a popular song of the time, which was to resound down through the years and decades: "and when they ask us / and they're certainly going to ask us / the reason why we didn't win the Croix de Guerre / oh we'll never tell them, we'll never tell them / there was a Front but damned if we knew where..."

Where was the Front and how do we proceed there? No sooner than we had crossed the street in front of the Mission building than we heard Spears' voice hailing us back as he shouted breathlessly from the entrance way of the chateaux: "Brigadier, Tilyard! Hold hard! Wait!" He bade us back, and we complied. He explained that he had just received a telegram which had literally fallen on his desk "would rather curtail your plans, am afraid.." We returned to Spears' office. He handed Dowding the piece of paper which brought the curtain down on his mini-adventure:

MOST URGENT TO BRITISH GHQ, PARIS FRANCE

FROM KENNARD , RAF FARNBOROUGH, ENGLAND

MINISTRY OF AIR REQUESTS BRIGADIER DOWD-ING IMMEDIATE RETURN PENDING TAKE-UP OF APPOINTMENT OFFICER COMMANDING AIR SQUADRON AT YORK MOST URGENT COMPLY FORTHWITH

In that moment, all the plans that had been formulating in this man's brilliantly turned strategic head to influence the course of what all those involved hoped was a shortening of the War, came to nothing. Not even a return to the Air Ministry but to the safety, anonymity and frustration of home duty far away from the action. Any lesser man would have registered shock, surprise, rage. He shrugged a shoulder,

"Well, gentlemen. The twists and turns of military life. I am ordered home and to York, of all places. We who would wish to command are also commanded."

"But sir," I began.

"No use, Tilyard. No 'but sirring'. Orders are orders, as not a few of us have taken extra pains, over a long while now, to explain to you. I am sure that your Headmaster, whatever else he may or nor have instilled at that unconventional establishment he ran, managed to convey the truth that we may lay our plans all we like but those powers beyond our understanding often have other plans. As for mine, they are to catch the next boat train out. The rather more pressing question is what we do with you, Tilyard..."

Major-General Spears, who had discreetly withdrawn from the room whilst this exchange took place, knowing its import, reappeared as if on cue.

"Don't worry about young Tilyard, sir. We can find him plenty to do. I can make use of him here, just forward the plans. I am only sorry that you have been rather thwarted in the dekko at the Front plan. Have you got time to stay for dinner? The last boat train out of Calais at this time of year is later than usual. Better still, stay the night, then go."

Dowding turned down the offer of dinner with "Nothing would give me greater pleasure than staying for dinner and accept your overnight hospitality, but it would, I fear, be a liberal interpretation of the word 'immediate'."

"Then at the very least, allow me to send for the car to convey you to the station for the train for Calais for the early evening boat. I'll get cook to rustle up a picnic supper. No arguing, Brigadier, this is my prerogative. I'll sort it soonest." He left, evidently giving us some time together before departure.

"Well young Tilyard, as Colonel Kennard might say, thy name is unconventional and thy progress a little mysterious. The next attachment awaits. Learn from this man, Edward Louis Spears. By all accounts he is as wayward as you, and not popular with the hierarchy, but does not seem to let it hinder him in his activities or the underlying way he conducts himself. I only pray that there is room enough for two of those peas in this military pod. Look, I know you'd rather come with me to the station for the boat-train and see me off, and I will not make it an order for you to stay but if you hold me in any regard, please respect my wishes and refrain. It would be too much of a reminder of what we may have done together, had we had time vouchsafed. We don't. Toby Kennard will have taken it as read you will be fixed with your next berth, whatever happens to him or I in the snakes and ladders of military affairs. That is what matters. Serve Spears and your joint work as well as I know you would have served ours, and I am certain you served Colonel Kennard."

Spears reappeared, again as if some line cue had summoned him, with a laden French-style picnic basket. "Ah, Brigadier. This should keep the wolf from the door on the journey. Chicken sandwiches, sausages, an apple tartine, made by the fair hand of Madame the Cook. Complete with a bottle of the local red and coffee in a flask."

With the intuition of a natural liaison officer and the mercurial emotional intelligence I was to come to know well, Spears made the next moment as smooth as it could have been, given one and all involved:

"Look, just before you go Brigadier, got a couple of matters to run by you, senior chap to senior chap as it were, begging young Tilyard's pardon of course. Will walk you the car, explain to my driver what's going on. You know how these chauffeurs for the duration can be sticklers for protocol! That all okay with you, Tilyard? Good, good."

Before I could respond the moment passed. Dowding and I exchanged glances. Dowding, Spears and I saluted, and the two senior officers turned to leave the office. I called after Dowding. "Sir, may your journey be swift, your arrival safe and your mission successful." He smiled, started as if to make a remark, thought better of it, glanced at Spears, and left the room without another word exchanged. What Spears knew then and I did not, hard as that decision appeared to me to be, was that I could watch the departure without having to confront the emotional impact directly. For that I was grateful, and it was to be perhaps one of the fondest memories I carried of him from that day to this – a kindness and an act of robust brotherly love for one officer towards another, a senior to a junior (and who knew of admiration and affection one for another).

On his return from seeing him off Edward Spears looked as many people did following an encounter with Hugh Dowding, however long or short, when they realised the mark of the man. "What an extraordinary man. He should be running the Supreme War Council not an aerodrome in the North of England." It was to happen in the unknowable future, to us then, that Dowding was to play a crucial role at the highest point of Britain's mortal danger in a war for survival to come but fall victim once again to infighting and bureaucratic turf battles.

Spears caught my hangdog expression and with a cheerful grin encouraged and chivvied me along, as indulgent seniors so often do their juniors, if inclined to the generous, as Spears was. "Look here, young man, no use moping with the might have been. We all have our orders and between them and the world having its way, we play our parts as best we can. Now, got something here which may interest you as a budding photographer..." He went to the drawer of the large ornate desk on which he worked and brought out a cardboard box, from which he produced what looked like a small metal box with a lens in the middle. It was the smallest camera I had ever seen. Spears smiled: "this is the future, my boy. No more enormous contraptions on legs but a machine for the hand. German designed, made by a company called Leica. Just think how it will transform the taking of pictures. The chaps at the propaganda bureau would give their eye teeth for one of these, I'll bet. Here, have a look..."

I took this wondrous machine, with the light of marvel in my eye. It was beautifully designed and so small. I asked the Major General where he acquired such a thing and he smiled enigmatically: "that is for me to know and you to guess at, save to say from one of our French comrades-in-arms, with whom as you know I am friendly, and he got it from a captured Boche. Now I pass it to you as perhaps a spoil of war that I have a feeling will come in useful..." He must have registered my mixed look of hesitancy and embarrassment at such an offer and eased the moment with characteristic aplomb. "At times, Tilyard, it is best to accept gifts gracefully and without demur. Worry not. Take it and use it with my blessing."

Yet as much as this mechanical wonder entranced me I could not help but think about where it had come from. How had the Frenchman who gave it to Spears come to possess it and under what circumstances, and who was this German whom he had taken it from? Who had manufactured this extraordinary device? For now, matters of where I was to spend the night, then find lodgings and other practical matters pressed for my attention.

One of these matters included how I was going to get to the Front. As if able to read my mind, Spears said: "I expect you are wondering if you'll ever get anywhere near the action. I wondered that when I was first appointed liaison, and have four wounds to prove how wrong I was. I realised early on that if a chap is charged with any kind of liaison duties between camps, he simply must go and see for himself what is going on and satisfy himself that what he reports back is out of his own experience and not third hand. When I was with the French generals in '14 and liaising with Sir John French and the BEF, it was my direct encounter with matters on the ground that enabled me to relay the concerns which stopped the BEF wipe out. I know you're keen to see for yourself. I'll see what I can do."

CHAPTER EIGHT

E dward Spears was as good as his word, and more so. He took me on a personal tour of the Front. It was to change my perspective on life and living profoundly. An incident there also left me with a scar on my forehead, above my left ear, as a permanent reminder of that day, (which happened to fall on the morning of the 11 November 1918). A sniper's bullet grazed my head as we walked on a trench duckboard. One move of my head to right or left I would have joined the brethren beneath Flanders' field "row on row" as the poet had it. Afterwards, as the nurse dressed the wound at a nearby field station Spears offered his usual consoling bonhomie. "Well now young Tilyard. You now have a badge of honour, a mark of true wartime liaison. Something to shut the buggers up at GHQ when they dare to cross-question you, and those that ask, in the years to come, what did you do during the conflict?"

So, I remained under the care and tutelage of Edward 'Louis' Spears. I was spared the mud and blood as a liaison officer attached to his staff at the British Military Mission. I came to be known as *Louis'*

Liaison, a term derived from the usual mixture of contempt, jealousy and admiration from brother officers unable to quite understand, or quite accept, my role in the unfolding drama of the denouement of the War to End all Wars. Dowding's fear that a Colonel of the line would hoist me into the trenches or a desperate wing commander of the newly-created RAF would send me aloft for air combat duty proved, happily for me, unfounded. The arrangement did not spare me, however, bearing witness to the carnage.

The autumn of 1918 was to prove as costly in lives, blood, misery and sheer human folly than any previous passage of time in the four-year slaughter. The so-called 'bloody April' of 1917 gave way in turn to 'black September' of 1918. Thousands of aircraft flew over the muddy carnage that now outlined northern France and Belgium, and hundreds of Allied planes shot down. In September alone over three hundred British, one hundred French and eighty-seven of our erstwhile American allies pilots and planes were lost. Black September indeed.

The destruction could be seen readily across the landscape and countryside of Northern France and Belgium, where the majority of the fighting took place: farmland laid waste by the men and machinery of industrial warfare; animals in their hundreds and thousands slaughtered; civilians uprooted; lives and livelihoods forever affected. Names of battlefields which would resonate down through the years: Ypres, Passchendaele, the Somme, Vimy Ridge, Looe; Gallipolli.

How to explain the scenes of carnage that met my naïve and hitherto sheltered mind? Later generations would come to see this great conflagration in sepia-tinted photographs or black and white images of relatives long dead or on that day that was to become known as

Remembrance Sunday, watch march pasts and poppy parades. It has cast a long shadow into the then-unknowable future. The war to end all wars was then just reaching its last gasp. The assassination of an Archduke in Sarajevo, then part of the Austro-Hungarian empire, had caused a chain of events which plunged Europe and the world into a conflict which raged for four years, spreading from France and Belgium to Africa, Asia and the Middle East, claiming millions of lives, as well as the war wounded and the further millions of lives blighted by fathers, sons, husbands, brothers who returned to families physically or mentally scarred, many never to fully recover. Families lost loved ones, fiancées lost future husbands and widows present ones, countries lost future leaders in all walks of life and Europe lost more than a generation of its youth to the bloodshed, if the unborn one is counted.

CHAPTER NINE

*" We were journeying to Paris, not merely to liquidate
the war, but to found a new order in Europe. We were
preparing not Peace only, but Eternal Peace. There was
about us the halo of some divine mission"*

Harold Nicolson (Peacemakers 1919)

After the guns fell silent, it was not long before Paris was a-buzz with the noise and bustle of a great meeting and the streets, bars, cafes and hotels resounded to the sound of plenipotentiaries and potentates, kings, chieftains and tribal leaders; ambassadors, prime ministers and advisers had all gathered to hammer out the Peace Treaty to end all Peace Treaties; to settle terms for the world following the War to end all Wars. The World in all its splendour and awesome majesty came to the City of Light to bind up its wounds, tell of its suffering and make some sort of peace with itself in the city which had just seen the light of the belle époque era shattered, extinguished by the sounds of the guns on the Western Front.

There were those in the city who professed the desire to beat swords into ploughshares, somewhat paradoxically, through force of arms if necessary. And behind the scenes – backstage as it were, where statesmen ply their trade, stood another army; of waitresses and cooks, valets and butlers' chauffeurs and private secretaries who served this mighty conversation. Providing the comforts of home to delegates and those who go hither and thither at their bidding. A hidden river flowing through hotel and guesthouse, restaurant and café paralleling the mighty Seine in its ebb and flow. These were the hundreds of diplomats, princes, potentates and plenipotentiaries of all the states on earth gathered in Paris for six months bargaining over and deciding the fate of millions.

It had been decreed by the powers re-making the world that nations should try and find a way to settle their disputes through negotiation and arbitration rather than force of arms. The ultimate symbol of this laudable aim was to be the League of Nations, born as a result of the idealism of President Wilson of the United States of America. My old headmaster would no doubt have approved of this approach, and indeed the Quaker-influenced education I had received under him would give me an insight into what drove these men who wanted to build a new world from the ruins of the old.

I encountered the figures re-shaping the modern world and saw them come and go about their business: Figures such as British Prime Minister David Lloyd-George, that mercurial, brilliant, fast-thinking Welshman who was as unconventional as he was mystifying; Georges Clemenceau of France, world-weary, cynical, deeply suspicious of both allies and enemies alike yet honest in his assessments of the

frailty of men; Orlando of Italy a product of the deep South of the
Italian peninsula attempting to face both ways at the same time on any
issue; and Wilson of the United States part preacher, part academic,
moralizer-in-chief with a penchant for ideals sustained by enormous
ambition and personal pride overlaid with self-certainty which could
prove a lethal combination. It was this mix of high ideals and petulance
(it was said of the President that he was a 'good hater') that launched
the worthy concepts of self-determination, open diplomacy, international conflict-resolution underpinned by international law into the
then known universe inhabited by states.

Among the hundreds of diplomats, aides and assorted advisers I encountered, courtesy of Major General Spears, was a British Foreign
Office official by the name of Harold Nicolson. Attached to the British
delegation we fell into an easy rapport, one Englishman with another
- 'sympatico' as the Italians say. Due to his proximity with the 'great
and the good' and still flush with the enthusiasm and idealism of one
caught up in the inner workings of the mission to abolish war and
create the mechanisms for eternal peace, he suggested I come and meet
a few 'fellows of like mind' and perhaps take a few photographs of
those 'at present in charge of the world'. And so it was that I entered
the salons of the mighty, camera in hand. One morning an invitation
to one of the hotels where the four powers met. Up some ornate stairs
and into a musty room and suddenly they were all there: Clemenceau,
mournful with drooping moustaches; Lloyd-George quicksilver and
pulsating with energy; President Wilson shining with the light of mission in his eye. Some of the photographs taken first for the newspapers
and magazines, then used later for collected editions, then reference
works and finally for posterity, were mine, taken with the Leica given
to me by Spears.

Unexpectedly, and all too suddenly, Major General Edward Louis Spears' time as a man of influence in the satellites of the higher commandery of the British Army came to an end: the political machinations of the representatives of the four powers at work in Paris that year of 1919 had Spears as one of the many political casualties. Having survived the Western Front, he could not resist the Versailles Effect. His service was no longer required, and he returned to an England that had never been his spiritual home, or his actual one for very long, rejected by those he had worked so hard to bring together in understanding if not amity: the British and the French commands. No-one, least of all those re-making the world in Paris could possibly have imagined that those very skills of liaison would once again be needed just two decades hence.

So, the time had come for the change in my association with Edward Louis Spears, the next man in the long chain of men who had such a powerful impact on my life. He had welcomed me into the brotherhood of those who liaise with the powerful and mighty, whether military, political or state. He taught me that an unconventional heart beneath a conventional exterior and an understanding of the culture of a still-stratified class-bound society could be an advantage in dealing with the myriad ways of men of affairs. Having re-fired my passion for photography, the developing art of the 20th Century, he showed me how I could observe the world through a lens and be part of the passing parade whilst coming to know its folly.

Indeed, through Spears' continued guidance and encouragement I took photographs: of uniformed and frock-coated men entering and leaving buildings and the squadrons of chauffeured cars and taxis waiting attendance; of the delegates from all over the known world bearing requests, demands, declarations; of the signatories to the peace

in the gilded halls of Versailles. I bore witness, to the making of the
Peace through the Treaty, of what became seen as the first act in a
tragedy six months in the making and twenty years in the unfolding.
Yet in life as in art, relationships and the wide array of human affairs,
what seems like a joy, a wonder, a beautiful moment can often turn
out later to be anything but. With hindsight we see the patterns of our
lives, which is just as well for if we knew what was to come, would
that not make life unbearable? We look through a glass darkly as the
poets and philosophers have long told us, but many is the time we
have looked in the glass and found a distorted picture. So, it was with
the peacemakers of 1919. How could they, and we who were there to
witness it, possibly know what was to come?

When the world powers concluded the peace at Versailles in the summer of 1919, it looked much like a settlement imposed on the defeated
by the victors. Nicolson the diplomat and diarist had it best when he
concluded that the "new order had merely fouled the old." There may
have been a League of Nations, embodying the hopes and aspirations
of nations speaking peace and concord to other nations but there were
also empire-power mandates which was not much less than ongoing
colonialism in another form, called by another name. So much for
President Wilson's fourteen principles underpinned by 'self-determination.' As was pointed out by wits and cynics, even the good Lord
only ordered Ten Commandments.

Yet these days were to cement my love of the city which in later decades
would be celebrated in song for the mass media age of movies and
radio, both of which would in due time claim my affections alongside
the art of capturing a moment stilled in time. In my middle age a
musical film version of the novels of French writer Colette charting
the adventures of courtesan-in-training *Gigi*, set in a Paris during the

belle époque which had been silenced by the guns of August 1914, written by an Anglophile American and a Viennese refugee captured the heart of it for me. It somehow blotted out the tragedy that was to come of the Paris under occupation by Germans two decades after the best efforts of Enlightened Man had attempted to outlaw war in Europe. Perhaps, then, now and always it was best summed up by the line known from a movie made in the heat of the Second Catastrophe of the Century, born from the First, when the hard-boiled American hero says to his love on renouncing her for the greater good: "we'll always have Paris."

When I left Paris, it was with a youthful optimism, tempered by experience, forged by proximity to a conflagration that had claimed millions of casualties yet untouched save for a scar which paid testament to a lucky fortune of war – the bullet that missed. Discharged from my military duties as His Majesty's armed forces no longer needed an over-promoted young liaison officer, the severance was eased by a payment of several hundred pounds and letter of introduction from the hand of Harold Nicolson, writer and diplomat to a friend in the British Embassy in Constantinople. During the course of our acquaintance, he had suggested that a "young man of your tendencies, interests and leanings should go East." Nicolson had been a diplomat in that city on the Bosphorus which was to become central to the unfolding drama being played out at the junction where Europe met Asia known as the final days of the Ottoman Empire. Three empires would fall as a result of the late war and the Treaty of Versailles would ensure the last rites were read in their capital cities – Berlin, Vienna and Constantinople. A man of biting wit who wielded a sharp stiletto pen bone dry with the trenchant observation of the failings of humanity including himself, Nicolson was also a man of impulsive generosity.

He not only furnished me with an introduction but also the means by which to travel east in comfort and style. In the last days of the world's residence in Paris, he accosted me one evening in the bar of the Hotel Majestic:

"Dear Boy, just the fellow. Now we have concluded our business here you are free to go. Gather you have the discharge in the pocket. I suggest you go east. Take that camera of yours and go and see for yourself the consequences of what we have wrought. What say you to a trip to Constantinople? I'll write to my old pal Harry Ponsonby at the Embassy."

"Well, sir, Mr. Nicolson that is well, very generous of you. I must confess I hadn't given much thought to what's next."

"You should young Tilyard, you should. Well appointed chap like you. I heard that a triumvirate of high ranking and influential fellows name of Kennard, Dowding and Spears thought very highly of you – shaver though you are of course! Don't look bashful, all true. Now look, the word is the old trans-continental train, the Orient Express is to start back in business. Runs from Paris to Constantinople via Germany, Austria, Romania and Bulgaria. Just so happens I have a pre-war diplomatic voucher-ticket all the way to the Sublime Porte. Won't be needing it as have been called away to work with Drummond in the League. It is yours, old boy, should you want it. Think it over, not too long mind as I have to pack bags for Geneva. If it appeals, I'll see you at the Gare de L'est tomorrow noon sharp. Don't look so shocked, Tilyard. Another adventure awaits. The answer, I rather fancy, should be yes, Mr. Nicolson, yes! I bid you bon soir, juenne homme, bon soir."

So, saying the next agent of my propulsion through the world took his leave of me and the barman with a characteristic flourish of glass flung back, double-breasted blazer buttoned and made for the door, the lobby, the stairs and his suite. I made my way across town to my modest lodgings and began to pack such belongings as I had acquired since first arriving in the city in the autumn of 1918. The uniform of a captain of Intelligence in the British Army folded into a cardboard case, representing an extraordinary passage, was replaced by the other 'uniform' that became the sartorial motif of my life, as it was my father's – roll-neck sweater, blazer, corduroy trousers. In the morning I bid farewell to my landlady who had cast a maternal eye over me, in the inimitable way of Parisian concierges, these past months. She would forever have a place in my heart. In years to come whenever I found myself in her arrondissement I would stand on the pavement opposite her building summoning the wherewithal to knock on the door. When finally, decades later, I finally summoned the courage to knock the door, the enquiry yielded a middle-aged woman looking strikingly similar to Madame Foulange - her niece. I was a year too late but that most indefatigable of women had left me a gift non pareil – an album of photographs documenting my non-consummated visits, and how the young man became an older one as the passing years showed. She knew me so well, perhaps best of all. She knew I would return to a spiritual home. The photographer photographed.

I set out for the Gare as I set out for the station at Reading in what seemed like a lifetime previously, but in fact was all of eighteen months, determined once again to do as I was bidden by my elders and seize the opportunity. Another station platform, teeming crowds, steam-filled concourse and another assertive, self-confident member of the British ruling class there to meet me in the form of Harold

Nicolson, standing at the ticket-end of the barrier, in homburg hat, overcoat and scarf:

"Ah, Tilyard! You decided to come. Good man. Something told me you would." From the inside pocket of his tailored jacket with something of a flourish he produced a docket of papers. Inside the docket a sealed envelope, the second of significance in my life, and a ticket voucher.

"Now, dear boy. Close attention, close attention. Needless to say, do not lose these. They are your safe passage and *carte bleu* as the French say. Letter of introduction to my pal Ponsonby at the British Embassy in Constantinople. Shall leave the usual conventions about not reading the contents of a missive from one gentleman to another entirely to your discretion."

Before I could respond with a grave "of course not" shrug Nicolson produced the most elaborate train ticket I had ever seen. Embossed with the mark of the Orient Express and endorsed by His Majesty's Foreign Office.

"This, my young giant is your passport to the East! Since you are travelling under the auspices of the FCO it entitles you to a First-Class berth, dining car access, all the way to the Sublime Porte..."

Once again I was, nearly, lost for words, "But Sir, Mr. Nicolson, sir how?

Nicolson seemed to brush that off and with an airy wave reached into his pocket withdrawing several large denomination notes in English and French currency:

"Ah, nearly forgot. Some spending money in lieu of military severance as you may want to stop off en route. As your erstwhile seniors would say, accept with grace, pay attention, report back when you can and travel safely... now off you go. The train awaits!"

The Orient Express, which was to establish itself through books, films, photographs, travel brochures in the consciousness of twentieth century popular culture, had been laid off for the duration of the war, which itself quickly became lodged in the public imagination as the Great War. A man who was to become prominent in politics in the ensuing decades, himself an officer late of the Western Front, by the name of Harold Macmillan spoke of the 'halcyon days' of his youth at Oxford before the guns of August 1914 ended the old world. He further asserted that those who had not been alive to know that vanished world could ever conceive of its delights – the seemingly endless 'golden summer' of the Edwardian era of garden parties, ladies with parasols, boating on the river with men sporting boaters and blazers, regattas and balls. So, as memory is often rose-tinted, it may have been. To us who had survived relatively unscathed in body and reasonably intact in mind, there was a yearning, a thirst, a desire to breathe the heady air of peace (if only for a while) and seize life. I shall be ever grateful to that complicated, passionate, emotional man of pen and public affairs, that he recognised a deep need for onward adventure, and ministered to it – although I had not the wherewithal to know it myself.

I climbed aboard a train comprised of midnight blue cars bearing the legend Simplon-Orient-Express. It was bound for Istanbul via Milan and Venice, Lausanne, Simplon Tunnel, Belgrade and Sofia. Having found my carriage and compartment I came across yet more paper in my jacket pocket. Another docket of tickets, this time for two seats in a box at one of the most celebrated lyric opera houses in Europe –

La Scala in Milan. A hand-written note attached that could only have come from the pen of my sponsor, dare I call him a friend, Harold Nicolson:

"Dear boy, for your further education in matters cultural. A night at the opera in Milano. Nothing like it. Look up my old friend Bettina de Angelis. She cannot resist the teatro, even if resistant to the charms of men!" Another characteristic gesture from a kind if inscrutable man – generous, witty, a little unconventional.

Another platform, another train, another farewell. And, of course, another beginning.

ACKNOWLEDGMENTS

To all those who taught me, worked with me, advised me, gave me hospitality unbounded, and showed concern about the future of the work in progress that is me. This is for you all past, present and future.

AFTERWORD- A REFLECTION ON THE FIRST WORLD WAR.

"The lamps are going out all over Europe. We shall not see them lit again in our lifetime". (Sir Edward Grey, British Foreign Secretary. August 1914.)

"In Flanders fields the poppies blow / Between the poppies row on row, / That mark our place; and in the sky / The larks, still bravely singing, fly / Scarce heard amid the guns below.

"We are the Dead. Short days ago / We lived, felt dawn, saw sunset glow / Loved, and were loved / And now we lie in Flanders fields.

"Take up our quarrel with the foe: / To you from failing hands we throw / The torch; be sure to throw it high. / If ye break faith with us who die / We shall not sleep, though poppies grow/ In Flanders fields "

(John McCrae, 1915)

Families lost loved ones, fiancées lost future husbands and widows present ones, countries lost future leaders in all walks of life and Europe lost more than a generation of its youth to the bloodshed, if the unborn one is counted.

The war that Jak Tilyard and his fellow members of the Twentieth Century Survivors Club were caught up in, is now itself more than a century old. He may be fictional but those he is drawn from were very real. Schools across the length and breadth of Britain bear testament to the fact that many of the soldiers on the Western Front were school leavers, often going straight from desk to the Front. Subaltern officers were often drawn from the ranks of these very young men who led companies of men in the trenches drawn from sections of society they would not necessarily have encountered so directly in peace-time. These encounters between privileged young men of the middle and upper classes and working men drawn from factory, mine and plough took place daily by the thousand over the four year duration of the Great War, and they were to change British society. Major figures in British public life of the succeeding decades of the century became aware of the condition of the men they led on the Western Front, and were radicalised into post-war political activity. Major CRE Attlee (Clement) became Labour Prime Minister in 1945, served at Gallipoli and Captain MH (Harold) Macmillan became Conservative Prime Minister in the 1950s and 1960s, served on the Western Front, as did future Conservative Foreign Secretary and Prime Minister Anthony Eden.

The assassination of an Archduke in Sarajevo, then part of the Austro-Hungarian empire, caused a chain of events which plunged Europe and the world into the cataclysm known as the First World War. The conflict raged for four years, spreading from France and Belgium to Africa, Asia and the Middle East, claiming millions of lives and causing empires to fall and the map of the then-known world to be re-drawn by the Paris Peace Conference which gave birth to the Treaty of Versailles; itself casting a long shadow across the century. The bare statistics of the war dead are eye-watering and still have the capacity to shock: the Germans 1,800,000; Russians 1,384,000; 1,290,000 Austria-Hungarians; 1,384,000 French; 743,000 British. These figures do not include the war wounded and the millions of lives blighted by fathers, sons, husbands, brothers who returned to families physically or mentally scarred, many never to fully recover. In short the war "toppled governments, humbled the mighty and overturned whole societies" (Margaret Macmillan, *Peacemakers – Six Months that Changed the World*, John Murray, 2001).

> **"For four years the most advanced nations in the world had poured out their men, their wealth, the fruits of their industry, science and technology, on a war that may have started by accident but was impossible to stop because the two sides were too evenly balanced." (Macmillan, 2001, p2)**

France and Britain had been rival powers for centuries and were united, at first uneasily, in the war by the binding of the Entente Cordiale and associated alliances. A little under one hundred years before the British Expeditionary Force (BEF) set out for France, Napoleon had been defeated at Waterloo (1815) bringing to an end a series of conflicts which spanned centuries, punctuated by fragile peace agreements

The United Kingdom of Great Britain and Northern Ireland and accompanying Empire and dependant overseas territories, upon which it was said that the sun never set, emerged from the carnage victorious, bruised and manifestly changed. As the historian and broadcaster Andrew Marr puts it:

> **"Though the war did not change everything about Britain's story, it changed a lot. During it, we discovered big government, high taxes, working women......after the war women could no longer be denied the vote....what used to be called 'high politics' – the doings of Cabinet ministers and parliamentary debates simply mattered less...people might still be patriotic but they could not be gaily patriotic in the old way." (Andrew Marr, *The Making of Modern Britain*, Pan Books, 2010).**

These were not the only changes brought to a tired, war-weary, embattled nation. The meaning of it all was debated, discussed, argued about, re-examined in succeeding decades and down through the generations to the present day. These arguments have been "fought out in plays and novels, television comedy programmes and documentaries and they continue still". (Marr, 2010, p.117)

An example of an artistic response, and contribution to the ongoing debate, to this human catastrophe and the sheer scale of those losses was vividly brought to the arrested attention of the British and international public alike by the art installation at the Tower of London in 2014 commemorating the centenary of the outbreak of the First World War, *Blood Swept Lands and Seas of Red*. Conceived by the artists Paul Cummins and Tom Piper the installation featured the laying of 888,246 ceramic poppies around the moat of the Tower of London with each poppy representing a fallen British or Colonial soldier; bearing in mind that soldiers from the far-flung British empirical colonies fought on the Western Front and other theatres of war with tens of thousands of casualties. An exact figure for the war dead in total will probably never be found, hence the power of the representative tomb of the unknown soldier in Westminster Abbey. The idea of one poppy for each of the fallen corresponds with the notion conceived by the creator of the Commonwealth War Graves Commission, Sir Fabian Ware: to have a memorial to the dead that stands regardless of rank whether headstone in a cemetery or name carved on a town cenotaph. Equality of memorial as a principle was established. This exercise in modern memory-making by Cummins and Piper, taking as it does the symbol of the poppy so well known across the century, has been as powerful a method of telling the story of the impact of the war on Britain and the empire as the many plays, films, paintings, books created in the century since.

The poem *In Flanders Fields* by a Canadian physician, killed in 1915, helped to forge the symbol of the poppy as an emblem of remembrance. It underlines the importance of the act of remembering the dead and is a once and future reminder of the connections between the past and the present as well as the obligation of the living toward the dead. To wider society it is also an aide memoire, if ever there was one required, that Flanders fields lay at the heart of the Western Front and the Western Front lay at the heart of the conflict and the seat of the destruction of much of Europe's pretensions of a "civilising mission to the world" (Macmillan, 2001 p2)

The impact of the First World War on France, or the Great War as it was known until the global conflagration between 1939-1945 brought about a change of general designation, cannot be easily separated from that of Belgium. It can be seen still across the landscape and countryside of Northern France and Belgium, where the majority of the fighting took place: farmland laid waste by the men and machinery of industrial warfare; animals in their hundreds and thousands slaughtered; civilians uprooted; lives and livelihoods forever affected. Row upon row of headstones in the Commonwealth War Graves cemeteries and burial sites and a landscape still littered with military detritus left in the ground in the shape of shrapnel, bombs and bullets – no to mention the occasional body. Names of battlefields which resonate down through the years: Ypres, Passchendaele, the Somme, Vimy Ridge, Loos. The effect, impact, meaning and significance of the events of 1914-1918 is as much debated, discussed and argued about in France today as in Britain, Germany, Russia or any other participating country.

It is difficult for a modern generation to look at the First World War without consideration of the Second World War. We know how the story unfolds in a way that those caught up in it could not. In France, as in Britain, major figures who were to play leading roles in the coming global conflict, which at that point was not inevitable – subsequent history being an unknown future – participated in the Great War and those experiences had a profound impact on France. In the words of a prophetic French general Ferdinand Foch, the Treaty of Versailles represented a twenty year armistice, not peace. Charles De Gaulle, who as a symbol of Free French resistance in the 1940s and later President of France and Philippe Petain, figurehead of the collaborationist Vichy government during the years of the German occupation of France in the 1940s, played their part on the Western Front: Petain as the hero of Verdun and De Gaulle as an as-yet unknown cavalry officer. Indeed, in many ways the rise of the Nationalist Right in France and the seeds of 'Petainism' and Vichy were sown in the mud of the Western Front and in the glittering halls of the Palace of Versailles.

Away from the conference halls and the deeds of what the Scots call the 'high hedians', what of the impact on the men who did the fighting and the dying in the great conflagration? Now that the last of the surviving veterans have died, their experience comes to us via letters, diaries, songs as well as poems. The culture and mores of the times were reflected in the armies which fought the war: in the case of Britain, Edwardian England and France, the Third Republic (which was to become so discredited in the years which followed). The British soldiers ('Tommies' as they were known by the German Army and who in return were known by the British as 'Fritz') made great use of parody in adapted versions of popular songs of the day. This was brought vividly to life in the seminal stage play *Oh! What a Lovely War*, originally produced by pioneering theatre impresario Joan Littlewood and later a film directed by celebrated actor Richard Attenborough, which depicted the events of the First World War through the eyes of those who fought it with the extended use of song, sketch and poem.

An example below gives something of the flavour: the song *Gassed Last Night*, is a mock-heroic/ironic view of the effects of the use of poison gas in trench warfare.

" Gassed last night and gassed the night before /

Going to get gassed tonight if we never get gassed any more. / When we're gassed we're sick as we can be, / 'Cos phosgene and mustard gas is much too much for me. / They're warning us, they're warning us, / One respirator for the four of us. / Thank your lucky stars that three of us can run, / So one of us can use it all alone " (lyrics from *Oh! What a Lovely War*, produced by Joan Littlewood and Theatre Workshop, 1963; film directed by Richard Attenborough, Paramount Pictures, 1969)

After the First World War, chemical weapons were banned as a weapon of war under an international treaty, known as the Geneva Protocol, in 1925.

Copyright – Imperial War Museum

An iconic image of the First World War by American painter John Singer Sargent.

'Gassed' shows in horrifying detail the aftermath of a gas attack on the Western Front in August 1918

Sources:

Cummins, P. and Piper T., 2014, *Blood Swept Lands and Seas of Red* (www.ssafa.org.uk)

Macmillan M., 2001. *Peacemakers – Six Months that Changed the World* :John Murray

Marr A., 2010. *The Making of Modern Britain* :Pan Books

McCrae, J., *In Flanders Fields*, 1915 (poem):Punch (http://www.greatwar.co.uk/poems/john-mccrae-in-flanders-fields.htm) (http://www.greatwar.co.uk/poems/poets/mccraearticle.htm)

Oh! What a Lovely War, 1969, Directed by Richard Attenborough, Paramount Pictures

http://user52571.vs.easily.co.uk/wp-content/uploads/2015/07/Oh-What-A-Lovely-War-Education-Pack.pdf

Sargent, JS., 1918 *Gassed* [painting], (London Imperial War Museum Collection)

Profile of Marshal Foch

http://www.history.com/topics/world-war-i/ferdinand-foch

The Commonwealth War Graves Commission (www.cwgc.org)

Imperial War Museum archives (http://www.iwm.org.uk/centenary)

The Geneva Protocol 1925

http://www.un.org/disarmament/WMD/Bio/1925GenevaProtocol.shtml

Printed in Great Britain
by Amazon